GNAT

SUSAN ALEXANDER

SUSAN ALEXANDER

Also by the author

The Snowdrop Mysteries:
The Ainswick Orange
The Snowdrop Crusade
A Remittance Man
The Heracles Project
St Margaret's
Beaumatin's Blonde
Hereford Crescent
Wolcum Yole

A Woman's Book of Rules

Illustration of Galanthus 'Gnat' by Freda Cox

GNAT

For Jean Jacques

and Diana

and with many thanks to Freda for "Gnat"

SUSAN ALEXANDER

Galanthus Gnat

A cultivar of G nivalis, Gnat is a miniature, a mere 10 cm in height.

The inner segments display the standard "Chinese bridge" mark. More distinctive are its outer segments, which are blunt and splayed. Hanging down like an insect's wings, they flutter in a breeze and mimic a swarm of the small insects after which this Galanthus is aptly named.

Unlike G. nivalis Pewsey Vale, whose bulbs increase vigorously and produce a plethora of leaves but few, if any, flowers, Gnat blooms prolifically and is arguably the best "good doer" of the miniatures.

Gnat's ovaries are elongated and pedicels are medium in length. Spathes bend slightly. Leaves are applanate, narrow and erect.

Gnat was discovered blooming in an old churchyard in Shropshire by Nat Marsh in 2011. It is being propagated and will soon be available commercially.

Susan Alexander

Chapter 1

"Be careful what you wish for," Maggie was thinking to herself as the discussion flowed on around her.

Maggie was having lunch with Thomas, her husband, and three friends. The friends were Stanley Einhorn, the famous hi-tech venture capitalist and billionaire, her Oxford colleague Chitta Kazi, who was getting married to Stanley the following week, and Malcolm Fortescue-Smythe, who owned The Global Press. His company had recently published a book Maggie had written and was about to bring out a second volume.

Maggie, known to the public as Professor Margaret Spence Eliot, had recently become the Weingarten Fellow at Merrion College, Oxford. The Weingarten chair had been established by Stanley in his mother's name. The position's responsibilities included organising the Weingarten lectures, a biannual event focussing on the developing world, and editing a series of books on related subjects the Global Press was also calling "The Developing World."

The tall, green-eyed American with unruly auburn curls had been on a sabbatical from her position at Oxford a year previously when writer's block had struck. Her friend Anne Brooks, the wife of a colleague and knowledgeable about such things, had proposed Maggie borrow a cottage in a small Cotswold village to be able to work with fewer distractions.

When that had failed to do the trick, Anne had insisted that what Maggie needed was a break and dragged her friend to a snowdrop study weekend at Rochford Manor. The Gloucestershire home of Lord and Lady Ainswick was famous for its woodlands that were carpeted by the small white flowers. During the weekend, Maggie had met Thomas and fallen in love. Not long after, she had married the man.

Getting married in itself would have been complicated enough for the post-menopausal academic, but Thomas also happened to be the 28th Baron Raynham and lived at Beaumatin, an estate in the Cotswolds that was also famous for its snowdrops and the grand, idiosyncratic house where Maggie now lived. At least when she didn't need to be in Oxford.

Which was why her new position as the Weingarten Fellow was so welcome, as it would allow her to undertake most of her work at Beaumatin. Trying to be two places at once the previous autumn had not been a happy experience for anyone and Maggie could only feel relieved by the new arrangement.

Tuning back into the discussion, Maggie heard it being unanimously decided that the first two books in the Developing World series would be a volume on the aftermath of colonialism by a Merrion colleague, Eunice Enderby, and a work on China co-written by another colleague, Stephen Draycott, and a professor he worked with in Beijing. In addition, the research Maggie and Chitta had done on the benefits of educating women in the third world and its impact on alleviating poverty would be also turned into a volume.

"And you need to think about what your next book is going to be," Malcolm reminded Maggie. The publisher was a handsome man in his fifties with the physique of an ex-rugby player.

"Next book? Can't we get my current opus launched before we talk about the next one?"

Maggie had written an academic volume during her sabbatical and Fortescue-Smythe had decided there would be interest in a more popular treatment of her work. In a few days, Maggie was facing a week of interviews and media appearances in London to publicize the new book.

"It's always good to plan ahead. And you know the sordid world of book publishing. It's always a case of 'What have you done for me lately,'" Malcolm reminded her.

Malcolm saw Maggie's startled expression.

"Or perhaps you don't," he amended.

Lunch had finished and Thomas excused himself.

"I also need to do some planning. Lady Ainswick is coming by to discuss the upcoming snowdrop seminars they are organising at Rochford Manor."

Lady Ainswick—Beatrix—and her husband Cedric were old friends of Thomas. They had also become friends of Maggie and she frequently turned to Beatrix for support and advice.

Thomas left and the group began to discuss Stanley's plans for the foundation he had established. The billionaire was in his early forties. Slight, of medium height, with thinning brown hair and pale, nearly colourless eyes, he had met Chitta the previous summer and immediately fallen head-over-heels for the beautiful Bangladeshi scholar.

Stanley and Chitta were going to undertake the day-to-day management of the foundation and Maggie would propose programmes for the foundation to undertake. Their first initiative would involve establishing free schools for girls in the world's poorest countries.

"I'd like to start in Bangladesh," stated Chitta, who knew what a difference such a school could make.

"And it looks like I will soon have some more money to contribute," said Stanley proudly.

"An investment I made is about to pay off. Big time. In a company called YuMi. Spelled Y-U-M-I but pronounced as though it were 'you' and 'me.' Stephen Draycott heard about it in China and alerted me. It's going to be the Chinese Facebook. But better. Better functionalities. Better look and feel. Two Chinese students at Stanford developed it. I got in on the ground floor and now it's going public this spring. But that's all I'm really allowed to say. Except…" he grinned at Chitta.

"Maybe I will finally feel it's time to retire from the VC business and devote most of my time to the foundation."

Maggie knew Chitta thought Stanley already had more than enough money, while Stanley's position was, "Can you ever really have too much money?" So this was interesting news and she hoped her friend would be pleased.

Maggie noticed cups were empty, so she left the table to ask the Beaumatin housekeeper, Mrs Cook, for some more coffee for herself and Malcolm and for some green tea for Chitta and Stanley.

Coming out of the dining room, she found Thomas in the great hall with Beatrix and her son-in-law David Osborne, who had taken over managing the gardens at Rochford Manor. Beatrix was in her mid-sixties, but Maggie thought she had been looking older and more tired since her daughter Chloe had married David and moved back home with her new husband.

David, a good-looking man in his early thirties, with curly brown hair and hazel eyes, seemed more energised. Both he and Chloe had worked at the Royal Botanic Gardens in Kew and Maggie concluded that he was enjoying his new responsibilities. He was also excited because Chloe was expecting in July.

Then a third person appeared. Someone Maggie knew.

She stared.

It was Nat Marsh.

Approaching fifty, Marsh was Maggie's height, with guarded grey eyes and dull, straw-coloured hair that always seemed to be a day beyond needing a shampoo and several weeks beyond needing a haircut. He had an expressive face that featured an aggressive nose, a strong jaw, a high forehead and eyebrows shaped like parentheses. Maggie had always thought his features were made for clown makeup.

But it was not the man's physical appearance that made Maggie unhappy to see him.

Marsh was a major personage in the world of galanthophiles, as snowdrop fanciers are called. He had "discovered" more than half a dozen new snowdrops and was an expert breeder of the small white flowers.

While it was Maggie's opinion that many of his finds had been poached from gardens whose owners were unaware that Marsh had made a discovery and of its value, that seemed to have little impact on the esteem in which he was held. And however he got his plants, Marsh successfully propagated them and then sold them at stratospheric prices to eager collectors. The most sought after he sold on eBay to the highest bidder.

Marsh was also paranoid, doubtless because he assumed others were as unscrupulous as himself. As a result, he not only never opened his garden to visitors, but also never even revealed its location. It was a secret as closely guarded as nuclear missile launch codes.

However, Maggie's real problem with the man was that she believed he had been behind the deaths of three people the previous summer. Which were the result of the thefts of some valuable snowdrops from Rochford Manor and the disappearance of half a dozen bulbs of Beaumatin's Blonde, a new snowdrop whose outer segments were liberally streaked with yellow that Thomas was propagating. Thomas had given six of the rare bulbs to the Ainswicks to plant at Rochford Manor for safety reasons. To not have all of his eggs in a single garden basket, so to speak.

Maggie had shared her suspicions with the police, but the detective she knew, Inspector Willis, had been satisfied with the obvious solutions. There was also no evidence connecting Marsh directly to the crimes. Just Maggie's intuition, which would not go very far in court.

Thomas was also impatient with Maggie's continued belief in Marsh's involvement. While he might not like the man, Marsh was widely respected for his accomplishments and expertise. He was a sought-after lecturer and his opinion highly valued.

So while Maggie was powerless to do anything about her suspicions, finding the man at Beaumatin was another matter. She would have liked to call Ned Thatcher, Thomas' estate foreman, and Ian and Wesley, who worked on the grounds, and have Marsh thrown out and the gates locked behind him.

However, Thomas was watching her closely, so she gave Beatrix a hug, welcomed David and nodded a greeting to Marsh.

Marsh nodded back, just as coolly. He was dressed as usual in worn corduroy pants, a plaid shirt, a shabby V-neck pullover and an ancient Barbour jacket. Over his shoulder he carried a Highgrove shopping bag. He never seemed to be without it and Maggie suspected he used it to carry away the snowdrops he poached.

"I'm on a quest to replenish our supplies of caffeine," she explained to Thomas.

"Perhaps you could ask Mrs Cook to bring coffee and tea to my study as well," said Thomas.

"Of course," she smiled. Maggie knew that both Beatrix and David liked Earl Grey tea. Coffee for Thomas, of course. As for Marsh, she didn't care what he preferred. Possibly a tisane of eye of newt. As far as she was concerned, he could make do with what the others were having.

At that moment, Freya and Loki, Beaumatin's two Tibetan mastiff guard dogs, came into the hall to check out the new arrivals. They recognised Beatrix and David, but stood still and regarded Marsh impassively. Then, perhaps because they sensed Maggie's feelings about the man or perhaps because they sensed something about the man himself, Freya put her ears back and Loki growled menacingly.

"What are those... those monsters?" Marsh asked in alarm and quickly positioned himself behind Beatrix.

"That's Loki and Freya. They're Tibetan mastiffs. Thomas got them to discourage snowdrop poachers," Maggie explained.

"Well, call them off. I'm no poacher," Marsh pleaded as Loki continued to growl.

Maggie, feeling that the point had been made, said, "Come Loki. Freya."

The dogs followed their mistress back to the kitchen.

Chapter 2

Malcolm was returning to London, while Stanley and Chitta were going to Pemberley, a nearby estate that Stanley had bought, renovated and named after Mr Darcy's property in *Pride and Prejudice*. Maggie went to check on Thomas and see if he wanted to say good-bye. She found him alone in his study. Beatrix, David and Marsh had already left.

"Would you like to bid our guests farewell?"

"Of course."

Thomas went into the hall to see off their friends. Malcolm had driven up from London in a vintage, bottle green Jaguar. Stanley, who could have driven any car he wanted, was showing off his newest purchase, a Skoda Yeti.

"Did you see that *Top Gear* episode? It was so cool. They actually landed a helicopter on the car's roof. While it was moving!"

Their guests departed and Maggie and Thomas returned back inside.

"My meeting went well. How was yours?" she asked.

Maggie was attempting a tone of casual inquiry.

Thomas looked at his wife thoughtfully. Finally he said, "Beatrix and David have organised two one-day seminars at Rochford Manor this year. David will lecture in the morning, then give a tour of their snowdrops. They'll lunch at the Rochford Inn, and then come here for a visit. I'll take the group through the gardens, with David and Marsh coming along to provide back-up. When that's done, they'll return to the Manor for a final talk by Marsh."

"Marsh is coming here with the group?" Maggie asked.

"Yes."

"Maybe he's hoping he can filch the remaining Beaumatin's Blondes."

As soon as she had spoken, Maggie wished she hadn't.

Thomas' mouth set in a thin line and she could feel the temperature plummet.

"Come with me," he said grimly. He took her arm and they went into his study. Maggie thought of it as Thomas' trying to get home court advantage. But she also appreciated that it meant they had their disagreements in private.

"You still have your fixation on Marsh? I hoped you had moved on."

"I am not fixated on Marsh. I hadn't even thought about him in weeks. Months, in fact. Until I suddenly find him standing in the hall here. In my home. If it's all right with you that I think of this as my home."

"I told you why he was here."

"That doesn't mean I have to like it."

"Maggie. You're acting like a… like some crackpot. There's absolutely no evidence Marsh was involved in those deaths. And thefts. The cases are closed. You need to forget about them. And him."

"I find it hard to forget about Charlotte Verney. I found her, you remember. With Emily."

Charlotte Verney was Beatrix's niece who had lived at Rochford Manor with her ten-year-old daughter. Maggie had found Charlotte hanging from a tree in the Manor's woods with Emily's arms wrapped around her mother's dangling legs.

Thomas did not want to think about that. Or be diverted.

"I need to be able to trust you not to make a scene when Marsh is here."

"I was polite."

"You were barely civil."

"I was cool. I learned that from you," Maggie pointed out.

Thomas glared. Maggie glared back.

She sighed.

"I promise I will not make a scene and be polite. All right?"

Thomas hesitated.

"Am I ever impolite? Do I ever make scenes?" she demanded.

Thomas had to concede that this was true.

"I'm not saying you have to like the man. I don't care for him much myself. But he's a highly respected member of the galanthophile community and Beatrix was fortunate that he agreed to come for the seminars."

Thomas felt that Maggie was still unconvinced.

"It's not like I'm asking him to come with us on vacation."

"Oh? Do you take vacations?"

Thomas' mouth twitched.

"Only when you drag me off on one, Papillon," he admitted.

Chapter 3

Maggie was drinking coffee with her friend, Anne Brooks, along with Derek Fiske and Damien Hawking, two garden designers who were also friends. Maggie had met Derek and Damien a year ago when she had accompanied Anne on the fateful Rochford Manor snowdrop study weekend.

Anne was an attractive woman close to Maggie's age with short brown hair expertly highlighted in half a dozen shades of honey and brown eyes. She was wearing jeans and a sweater patterned in lime green and dark blue. Derek and Damien were in their mid-thirties and were also wearing jeans, with plaid flannel shirts.

They were in the kitchen of Anne's Georgian home in Broadway. Derek, Damien and Anne were all excited about having been invited to the Snowdrop Ball by Thomas and the Ainswicks. The annual dinner and dance was being held in London and was going to be white tie.

"You two are lucky," Anne said to Derek and Damien. "You know how you're supposed to be outfitted. At least if you're wearing the traditional white tie and tails."

She paused.

"You are, aren't you?"

"Don't worry, Anne. We won't let the side down. I already have tails and Derek visited a tailor in Oxford last week and was fitted for his own set." Damien was reassuring.

"And it's a good thing that business has been good," said Derek with feeling.

"And what are you wearing, Anne?" Damien asked.

"Well, I already have a couple of gowns, from when I have to accompany Laurence to feast nights at Merrion. But I've been thinking about getting something new. It is going to be a very ritzy evening, since it's being held at the Dorchester and all. And then I can wear the dress at Oxford as well. The college's Master, Alastair Carrington, is retiring and I know there are some grand events being planned."

"And what are you wearing, Maggie?" asked Derek.

"I suspect Maggie has been haunting the Neiman Marcus website for the past several weeks," said Anne.

"Right, Maggie?"

Anne noticed that Maggie was no longer with them.

"Maggie?"

"Oh, I'm sorry. I, er…"

"Maggie, are you worried about something?" Anne asked shrewdly.

Maggie hesitated, then said. "Yes. Yes I am. And it's not about what I'm wearing to the ball. It's something else entirely. It's… Nat Marsh."

"Nat Marsh?" said Anne, thinking the name seemed familiar.

"Nat Marsh, the snowdropiteer? Auctions his bulbs on eBay?" Derek asked.

"Nat Marsh, discoverer of Galanthus 'Android,' so called because the inner green markings look like a little robot?" said Damien.

"At least they do if you close one eye and squint at it with the other," added Derek.

"And the double yellow 'Serena Marsh,' named after his mother," continued Damien.

"If you'd ever met Mother Serena, you'd know she explains a lot about our Nat," commented Derek.

"And Galanthus 'Lazy Boy,' because the flowers have an unfortunate tendency to flop over onto the ground," added Damien.

"That one's never been very popular with our clients," Derek pointed out.

"And finally 'Marsh's 'Amazon.' A very rare double with beautiful green streaking on the outer segments. It was being propagated by a professional breeder when suddenly the entire lot was wiped out by botrytis," Damien concluded.

"And Marsh just happened to have two bulbs, which he says he received as a gift from General Nigel Arbuthnot, in whose garden the snowdrop was originally discovered. Conveniently, because Arbuthnot had subsequently passed away and so couldn't verify Marsh's claim," said Derek.

"The paranoid Nat Marsh who never opens his garden to visitors for fear they'll poach his plants?" added Damien.

"So paranoid that he's never even let anyone know where his garden is?" finished Derek.

"That's him," Maggie agreed.

"Oh. Right. Isn't he speaking at the Rochford Manor snowdrop seminar this year? I've already signed up." Anne said.

"Us too," said Derek.

"And we've invited a couple of clients," added Damien.

"Yes. In fact, the Ainswicks are having two snowdrop seminars this year and he's speaking at both. On 'Developing a Snowdrop Collection.' And he's bringing the groups to Beaumatin for a tour of the gardens."

"So what's the problem?" Anne asked.

Maggie quickly decided she was not going to go into the deaths of Charlotte Verney, Linda Walker and Nick Greenaway. So she said, "I don't trust him. I think he's…. a bad man. A really bad man. But Thomas…"

"Thomas thinks Marsh is a pillar of the galanthophile set and won't hear a word against him," concluded Damien.

"Exactly," said Maggie.

"Even though he's not exactly what his lordship would call a gent," Derek pointed out.

"Yes. For some reason, that doesn't seem to make a difference the way it usually would," Maggie agreed.

"So what worries you?" asked Anne.

Maggie sighed.

"All right. I'll tell you. I think Marsh stole several 'Beaumatin Blonde's. Or I should say he got Nick Greenaway, who was briefly in charge of the gardens at Rochford Manor, to steal them. Back in August. And Beaumatin's Blonde? It's unique. Spectacular. It's a snowdrop with yellow not just on the ovary and the inner segments, but with pronounced yellow streaking on the outer segments as well. Sort of like Green Tear, but with yellow where the green is.

"And I'm worried it will turn up on eBay as Marsh's Golden Shower…"

Derek tittered.

"I know. Tell me. Or something similar. And it will get really ugly."

And that doesn't even begin to take account of the three people who are dead, Maggie thought, but did not say.

"So how can we help?" asked Anne.

"Yes. What can we do?" Damien seconded.

Maggie took a deep breath.

"I want to go to Marsh's secret garden and see if he actually has the Beaumatin's Blondes growing there. And check to see if he has anything else that he shouldn't. Like some other snowdrops that went missing from Rochford Manor at the same time. This is the right time of year to find out. When the snowdrops are in bloom."

"But no one knows where the garden is," protested Derek.

"It's Britain's best kept secret," agreed Damien.

"But maybe that's only because no one has tried to find it hard enough. Or used the proper technology," Maggie said.

Derek and Damien exchanged glances.

"And you think the perfect time to do that will be when we know he'll be at Rochford Manor," Anne concluded.

"Yes. And I'll be in London promoting the new book just before that. While I'm there, I'll see if I can acquire some, um, technological support. Maybe some other sorts of assistance as well. But it would still be helpful if you could keep an eye on Marsh while I'm, er…"

"Breaking and entering?" finished Derek.

Maggie grimaced.

"And don't forget the Rottweilers," added Damien.

"Rottweilers?"

"Talk is he has his place protected by Rottweilers. Really vicious ones. And scanners that read your retina before the gates will open. And a system of laser beams around the snowdrops that set off alarms when they're broken. And motion detectors. And…"

"Stop! This is Nat Marsh's secret garden, not an episode of *Mission Impossible*. And certainly all of his thefts, if I'm correct, were definitely low tech. He took advantage of human weakness and being presented with an opportunity, not high-end equipment. And as for the Rottweilers. Maybe. But maybe not. He was quite wary of Freya and Loki when he was at Beaumatin."

"That's not surprising. Everyone's scared of Freya and Loki," said Derek with feeling.

"Well, that's the point. And they don't frighten me," said Maggie defensively.

"Yes, but they like you. Or I assume they like you. It's hard to tell with those beasts," Damien pointed out.

Maggie laughed. "I know. They do tend to keep things low key. Unless they get upset."

"Which, frankly, is something I hope never to see," said Damien.

Derek nodded vigorously in agreement.

"But can I count on your help?"

"Of course," said Damien.

"Oh goody. Another Maggie adventure," said Derek.

"Another adventure," echoed Anne. "Just what we need."

Susan Alexander

Chapter 4

Maggie was thoughtful as she drove back to Beaumatin. While she may have been dismissive of Damien's and Derek's reports of guard dogs and retinal scanners, she certainly did not want to act foolishly.

Therefore, as soon as she was in the privacy of her study, Maggie called a man in London she knew named Tim. She had worked with Tim in the past when she had been consulting to the British government on immigration issues. However, since then, she had the impression he had moved to another department. Something involving national security. Or terrorism. Or… Whatever it was, Tim wasn't telling and Maggie knew better than to ask. However, she hoped he might be helpful with her Nat Marsh problem.

"Hi, Tim. It's Maggie. Eliot. Er, Raynham."

"Hello, Maggie. What a pleasant surprise."

"I'm glad it's pleasant, Tim."

"I trust you are not calling about any more drug traffickers?"

"No. No, they seem to have decided that there are better places to operate than the Cotswolds."

"I'm glad of that. And so…"

"I'm going to be in London next week. I have a new book coming out that I'm, er, promoting. And I wanted to know if you'd be free to have lunch."

"Let me check."

There was a pause and Maggie heard keys taping.

"I could meet you on the twelfth or the thirteenth."

Maggie checked her own schedule.

"The thirteenth would work. Is there any place you could suggest?"

"Do you know the Royal Thames Yacht Club? Knightsbridge? Next to the Mandarin Oriental?"

"That would be perfect. My publisher has booked me into the Mandarin Oriental."

"Shall we say noon, then?"

"Noon is fine. Thank you, Tim."

"Since I assume this request is not just that you miss mes beaux yeux, I must confess I am curious to see what Professor Eliot, aka Lady Raynham, is up to."

Maggie sighed.

Chapter 5

Maggie found it strange that a place called the Royal Thames Yacht Club was located on bustling Knightsbridge. There was no water in sight, let alone yachts, but perhaps Tim could explain.

Tim was waiting for her in reception. He was around Maggie's own age and just short of her 5'11". As usual, his moustache was meticulously groomed and he wore a good grey suit. He looked typically unobtrusive, but was obviously known to the club's staff.

"Tim."

"Maggie."

Maggie looked around. There were portraits of naval notables on the walls and other items of nautical memorabilia were on display.

"You can leave your coat in the Ladies' Cloak Room. It's past the stairs on the right."

Maggie nodded. She saw more portraits of the admiralty, more rudders, some oars and a wonderful model of a frigate under full sale. She wondered if Thomas' second son James, who was a Commodore in the Royal Navy, knew this place. She'd have to ask. She'd see him at the Snowdrop Ball, which was the following week.

She rejoined Tim.

"We're lunching upstairs in the Coffee Room. The food is quite good, as are the wines."

Maggie admired the view of Hyde Park. She ordered a plate of smoked salmon and some white wine, while Tim had traditional British roast beef and claret.

They discussed the book launch.

"I thought the one you did at the end of last year was excellent. If we had policies that reflected your findings, I would have less work to do," Tim commented.

Since Maggie remained unsure about what exactly Tim's work was, she simply nodded.

When they had finished eating and coffee had been served, Tim sat back and asked, "So Maggie. While I am always happy to see you, I suspect you have some reason for asking for this meeting. What would it be?"

"Oh dear. Yes. Well, I agree it is nice to catch up, but you're right. I do have a reason."

Maggie looked around. There were no other diners within earshot.

"Is it safe to... discuss something slightly problematic? I don't want to be indiscrete."

"Given the identities of some of our members, we are regularly swept for bugs and have taken precautions against hackers. So yes, please, speak freely."

"All right. Well. I need to, um, break into someplace. A garden, not a house. And I have no idea what kind of security it has. Dogs. Retinal scanners. Laser alarms. Motion detectors. No one is sure. It's just rumour. But I thought you might know someone... who had those kinds of skills... and could be hired..."

Tim laughed.

"Maggie Eliot. What have you gotten yourself into? You'll need to tell me a bit more before I decide whether I'm willing to help you."

So Maggie told him about Nick Greenaway. And Charlotte Verney. And Linda Walker. And the Beaumatin's Blondes. And the troubles at Rochford Manor.

"Everyone's decided that Charlotte's death was a suicide and that Greenaway murdered Walker and that he was behind the snowdrop thefts as well. But he's dead, so it's not like he can say anything to defend himself. But I believe it was someone else. Who was behind everything. And who's still, um, could you say, at large? And I'd hoped if I could get into his garden. See if he did have those Beaumatin's Blondes. And maybe some of the other valuable snowdrops that went missing from Rochford Manor."

Maggie explained about Nat Marsh. His status in the galanthophile community. His secretiveness and paranoia.

"He auctions his rarer bulbs on eBay for hundreds of pounds. And while I know snowdrop poachers are a genuine problem and he might be justified in being protective, I just feel…"

"And you couldn't tell your tame police inspector about your concerns and have him check out this Marsh?"

Maggie wanted to protest Tim's wording but decided that would be counterproductive.

"Willis? He is also convinced it was all Greenaway. And I admit there was no direct evidence implicating Marsh. But Tim. Three deaths. Plus the thefts. And the possibility of it continuing. Don't you think it should at least be checked out?

"If I'm wrong, if I'm just being fanciful, well, then that's that. Marsh is just an eccentric. And that's not against the law. But three deaths, Tim. And Charlotte left a young daughter. Emily. Who's now an orphan."

Tim leaned back, steepled his fingers and looked at Maggie. She looked back and he admired her deep green eyes.

"You realise what you're considering is, simply stated, illegal. If you get caught, there'll be nothing I can do. You'll have to rely on the mercies of your Inspector Willis."

"I know. I know. That's why I wanted to talk to you, to see if you might know someone who could assess the situation, rather than my just blundering in on my own."

Tim raised his eyebrows. "You thought I'd know someone who would undertake an illegal operation?"

Maggie gestured apologetically.

"We know where Marsh will be on Monday the eighteenth. And Monday the twenty-fifth. He's giving a lecture on snowdrops at a Rochford Manor snowdrop seminar. And then bringing the group for a tour of Beaumatin. I have friends who have signed up. So we can be sure where he'll be. And that he won't be at his place."

"Which you still have to discover."

"Yes. But I thought… a tracking device on his car?"

"Maggie Eliot. I am shocked! Shocked! That a respectable professor, not to mention the wife of a peer of the realm, would even think of such a thing."

Maggie started to apologize, then realised Tim was teasing.

"Let me make some enquiries. About this Marsh. And also, it is just possible I know someone with the, er, skillset you require. How long will you be in London?"

"Through Friday. And I'll be back on the twentieth."

"Ah. The Royal Horticultural Society Winter Show."

"Yes. How do you…"

"My mother never misses it."

Maggie had to smile.

"If you get a call from someone who asks you, hmm, whether the Ainswick Orange has been found, I suggest you say yes, in a field near Rochford Manor. Then you can arrange a meeting."

Maggie laughed at this. "Very cloak and dagger."

Tim became solemn. "Maggie, you want to do something that can get you into legal difficulties if you're caught. That could have consequences you wouldn't like. And your baron would be unhappy about it as well. Since I assume trying to talk you out of this is futile, I at least hope you are going to take this seriously. And be very careful."

Maggie nodded.

"Then expect a call. Or not. Depending on what I find out."

"Thank you, Tim."

They stood, hugged and walked off in opposite directions. And Maggie realised she had forgotten to ask about the yachts.

SUSAN ALEXANDER

Chapter 6

The next afternoon, Maggie had just finished an interview with a reporter from the *Financial Times*, when her mobile rang.

"Hello?"

"Hello," said a stranger's voice. "I wonder if you could tell me if the Ainswick Orange has been found."

Oh my. Maggie frantically tried to think of the agreed response. Whew.

"Yes. In a field near Rochford Manor."

There was a pause.

"Professor Eliot?"

"Yes?"

"A mutual friend suggested I call you."

"Yes. Your question about the Ainswick Orange kind of gave that away."

There was another pause.

"And arrange a meeting."

"Sorry. I'm a bit nervous about all this. Yes. A meeting. What do you suggest?"

"What is your schedule like for the rest of the day?"

"I'm free, actually."

"How about the bar at the Dorchester at seven."

"The Dorchester?"

"Yes. I assume you know where that is."

"I do, but isn't it a bit conspicuous?"

"You think if I suggested meeting in a pub in Brixton you'd be inconspicuous?"

Maggie had to admit the man had a point.

"Right. The bar at the Dorchester at seven. Um, how will we recognize each other? Should I carry a red rose?"

"Do you want to look like you're meeting someone from an online dating site?"

"No."

"Anyway, I know what you look like. And I'll ask you about the Ainswick Orange again."

"All right."

The stranger ended the call. Maggie looked at her mobile but the number he had used to call her was blocked. Tim's, er, agent had what her niece Brooke would call a "posh accent." Beyond that, she wondered what he would look like. Well, apparently he knew what she looked like. No mystery there. She was well represented on Google images. Especially with the attention her books were getting. And with her hair and height... Well, hard to miss.

She checked her watch. Four o'clock. She was in a Starbucks on Aldwych. What should she do until seven? Knightsbridge, she decided. Harvey Nichols. Harrods. More coffee.

Having replenished her scent—it was always good to have a backup—and enjoyed a cappuccino, Maggie took a taxi to the Dorchester. She was early. She was nervous. She would have a glass of wine while she waited.

The bar was packed. Glamorous fashionistas and men who looked like they thought they were the Masters of the Universe. Maggie remembered that Mayfair was where many hedge funds were based, so perhaps they were. She felt old. Dowdy, even though she was wearing a chic new suit by a famous designer she had gotten for her book launch.

And it was Valentine's Day, she suddenly remembered. She had left a card for Thomas with Mrs Cook. Simple. Unsentimental. No mushy doggerel. She wasn't sure what the baronial tradition was concerning Valentine's Day and she had almost never celebrated it.

A man approached. Thirties. Bespoke suit. One of the Masters of the Universe.

"Professor Eliot?"

Maggie nodded and waited for the question about the Ainswick Orange. To her surprise, he extended a copy of her book.

"I wondered if I could ask you to autograph this."

Oh. This was something new.

"Um… of course. How would you like me to sign it?"

"I have finally met the man of my dreams. Your ever-loving Maggie."

He extended an expensive fountain pen.

Maggie raised her eyebrows and channelled Thomas.

"Sorry. Just joking. To Josh would be fine."

Maggie signed and handed back the book and pen.

"And if you ever want to find out if I am that man…" he smiled wickedly.

"Josh," Maggie said, in a tone she normally reserved for undergraduates.

"Um. Right." Josh retreated into the crowd.

"Giving out autographs?" said a voice Maggie thought she recognised.

Maggie looked. The man was in his forties, ruggedly handsome with hard blue eyes and short brown hair that was artfully dishevelled. He wore a dark blue suit that fit him perfectly, despite his obvious muscles. He sat down at her table.

"Ainswick Orange. See, no roses were necessary."

"No. I guess the hair is enough," Maggie gestured to her curls that were escaping from her hairclip, as usual.

The man nodded.

"So. You are?"

"Crispin."

"Crispin…."

"Crispin will do."

Maggie was going to make a remark when she remembered she needed this man's help. Or she thought she did. Or at least Tim thought that this Crispin could help her.

"Crispin. Fine."

A waiter approached.

"Laphroaig, please."

"Water? Ice?"

"No. Just plain. Please. And will you have another?" Crispin indicated Maggie's near-empty glass.

"Viognier. Yes, please."

They people-watched until the waiter returned with their drinks.

"So, Maggie," Crispin toasted her.

"So, Crispin." Maggie did the same.

"I'm sorry. I feel quite awkward. I've never done anything like this. What did, er, Tim tell you?"

"He gave me the copies of the files on your deaths. Charlotte Verney. Linda Walker. Nick Greenaway. He gave me the file on you..."

"I have a file?"

Crispin grinned. It was a very attractive grin.

"A thick one, too. And one on Nat Marsh. That was much thinner. Nothing much to it."

"Nat has a file?"

"Anyone who sells a small white flower for hundreds of pounds is going to get someone's attention."

"All right."

"And one on that husband of yours."

"Thomas?"

"Shh, but all peers have files. Tim wanted me to know what I was up against."

"Up against?"

Crispin, or whatever his name was, grinned his infectious grin again.

"I gather his lordship does not share your views. About Marsh."

Maggie sighed. "No."

"If he did, he probably would have contacted his friend at Scotland Yard. Paul Dexter."

"True," Maggie agreed while being aware Crispin was showing off what he knew.

"Do I get to see your file?"

Crispin drained his whisky and grinned again. "Sorry. Classified."

He signalled to the waiter for another.

"Very well, then. As I understand the mission, you want to track this Marsh to his secret lair and find out if he has any stolen snowdrops."

"Yes. Not exactly the stuff of a James Bond movie."

Maggie paused.

"The file didn't say where the garden was, by any chance?" she asked hopefully.

"No. It just has his home address. Assuming where he lives and his garden are in different places."

"No. Definitely not the same place. Too bad. Well then, the first thing to do would be to find his garden."

Crispin nodded.

"And then… to get in and check out the snowdrops."

"Tim indicated that was the plan."

"While there are rumours he has heavy security—including attack dogs—I never had the feeling he had the resources. I mean, I would think laser alarm systems and retinal scanners don't come cheap. And we have Tibetan mastiffs at Beaumatin and he seemed, well, quite uncomfortable with them. I got the impression he doesn't like dogs much."

"Tibetan mastiffs?"

"Loki and Freya. To discourage snowdrop poachers."

"I would think they would."

"They're quite sweet if they know you."

Crispin looked sceptical.

"I'll have to tell Tim to add that factoid to your file."

Maggie gave Crispin a "give me a break" look.

"So… what do we do next?"

"*We* do nothing. *I* will try to find out where this Nat's secret garden is located. Tim seemed to think you know his schedule."

"Yes. At least on certain days. And there will be people I know who can keep their eyes on him."

"I can track his car. I gather it's snowdrop season, so the chances he'll go to his garden are high, presumably."

Maggie nodded.

"And I'm going to enlist the aid of a colleague. Name of Pilchard, Fred Pilchard."

"Pilchard? Really?"

"It seemed like it might be good to have some back-up."

Crispin sipped some of his whisky.

"Once we find out where the garden is, I can check out what kind of security Marsh has. Then, when you're sure there's no danger of his appearing, I can go check for those flowers of yours."

"Crispin, I'm fine with your tracking Marsh's car. And finding the garden. And determining what kind of security we're up against. But I seriously doubt you know a Green Tear from a Pusey Green Tips. Or a Hippolyta from an Ophelia. Or a Trumps from a Trym. Or a Mighty Atom from a…"

Crispin held up his hands.

"All right. I'm not going to argue with you. One thing at a time."

"Fine. One thing at a time."

Crispin took a swallow of his Laphroaig and regarded the glass appreciatively.

He really was very good looking, Maggie thought.

"So how does this work? Do you have a fixed fee? Or an hourly rate?"

Crispin shook his head. "This one's for Tim. I owe him."

"But…"

"Not subject to discussion."

Maggie sighed.

"How do you know Tim?" Maggie asked.

"I worked in his, er, department for some years. When they began cutting budgets, I took their golden handshake and became an, um, consultant. Fewer hours. Bigger fees. But they don't have to cover my pension or vacation days or private health care, so some bean counter figured this was cheaper."

"And you know about things like tracking cars. And retinal scanners."

"Among other things," Crispin grinned.

"Other things?"

"If I told you, I'd have to kill you."

"Right."

"Sorry. I couldn't resist."

Crispin finished his whisky.

"So tell me. Why does this matter to you?"

"Besides that I think he stole six of Beaumatin's rarest snowdrop? It's Emily. Charlotte's daughter. She's eleven. She found her mother. Hanging from a tree. She was already a bit... fragile. Now she's... well. Charlotte's death was ruled a suicide. I'd like to be able to tell her it wasn't. That her mother never would have left her. Not like that."

"All right. I can understand that."

"So what next?"

"If you could send me this Marsh's schedule. Where you're expecting him to be. And when."

"I know some of it already. Not all. But enough. He'll be in Gloucestershire this coming Monday and the Monday after that. And in London at the end of next week. And as you said, it's snowdrop season, so he'll need to visit his secret garden. I tend to think it's someplace in the Cotswolds. Well, it can't be too far from his home in Oxfordshire."

Crispin grimaced. "The provinces?"

"The Cotswolds are very civilised."

"If you say so."

"And Oxford's in Oxfordshire."

"That I do know."

"How do I let you know his exact schedule?"

"Aha. Here."

Crispin reached into his briefcase and removed a small box.

"Use this to call me. My number is on speed dial. *1."

Maggie shook her head.

"Like I told Tim. Very cloak and dagger."

"And I believe he told you that what we're doing is illegal. So no SMSs. Just voice. The number is untraceable. But be discrete anyway. In case things go wrong, I want as little evidence as possible."

Maggie sighed.

"You're right. I'm sorry. And I am taking this seriously, I promise."

"I hope so."

Tim looked at their empty glasses.

"One more round?"

Maggie was tempted.

"I'd better not. I have to prepare for tomorrow. And call Thomas."

"Ah. His lordship.

"Yes. He's not very happy when I have drinks with men in bars. Even when it's for a righteous purpose."

Crispin grinned. And ordered another Laphroaig.'

"And Thomas definitely does not support my theories about Marsh. In fact, he thinks I'm obsessed. Fixated. And he gets very, um, cranky when I express my discomfort about letting Marsh run free at Beaumatin. And Rochford Manor. With his ubiquitous Highgrove bag. You know, like the ones you get to carry home your groceries? Or library books? Reusable? Save the planet? And which I suspect Marsh uses to ferret away the snowdrops he poaches.

"If only there were a forensic test that would tell exactly which snowdrops had been in his bag. But apparently the DNA of one snowdrop is very like another. Whether it's worth four hundred pounds or four."

"But soil can be very precisely identified," Crispin pointed out.

"It can?" Maggie brightened. "Well, that would be something. Even if Marsh has planted the snowdrops he's taken in his secret garden, I imagine some bits of soil from their origins could still be found on the bulbs. Or traces would still be in his bag."

Crispin grimaced.

"Forensics? That might be over our budget. But first things first. Which is finding this secret garden of yours."

"Yes. Or Marsh's, actually. That would certainly be a good first step."

Crispin took a swallow of his whisky.

"How is your book launch going?"

Maggie grimaced. "The liberals think I'm proposing the infringement of basic human rights. The conservatives think I'm anti-immigration. And they both think I'm anti-Islam. None of which is true. And I'm not convinced anyone has actually read the book."

Crispin surprised her by saying, "I read it. I think it's good. I'm not sure I would outlaw niqabs and burqas, but as far as language and education, I agree."

"But niqabs... Well, I shouldn't get started. But thank you. And The Global Press, my publisher, is happy about the sales. So I guess that's something."

"Sales. Yes. In the end, I guess that's what it all comes down to."

Maggie shook her head.

"Anyhow I should be going. Let me…"

She went to gesture for the bill but Crispin caught her hand. Held it.

"That's all right. Tim said the drinks are on him as well."

"But…"

"Think of it as the thanks of a grateful nation. And I gather they have some reasons to be grateful."

"Hardly."

"And I've seen your impressive financials, so it's not like I think you're a poor professor and can't afford this."

"What?"

"Also in the aforementioned file."

"Really?" Maggie was indignant.

"You're not so naïve as to think Her Majesty's government would consult with someone without checking out him or, in this case, her pretty thoroughly first?"

Maggie sighed. Perhaps she was naïve, as Thomas had reminded her more than once in recent months.

"Well, thank you. Or thank you, Tim. Anyhow, I must go. And I'll get you that information."

Crispin stood.

"It was a pleasure to meet you." Maggie extended her hand.

Crispin took it, used it to pull her towards him, and kissed her on the cheek.

"The pleasure was all mine," he said, grinning.

Chapter 7

The snowdrops were in full bloom at Beaumatin. Clumps of Wendy's Gold drew the eye with their sassy yellow ovaries, while more reserved Lady Elphinstone required the curious to lift her head to see her double yellow petticoat. Tiny Elfin clustered charmingly and, with his long pedicel, Magnet bobbled in the slightest breeze.

Thomas proposed Maggie join him for a garden tour. As they walked, Maggie tried to identify the different cultivars before checking their labels. She succeeded with about a fourth. Which would not have merited at pass at Oxford, but was still a great improvement from the none-at-all it would have been a year earlier.

Thomas squatted down. He took a snowdrop between two fingers and deftly turned it up to better see its inner segments.

"It's Grumpy. Do you remember Grumpy?" He looked up at Maggie and his eyes were warm.

Maggie remembered Grumpy. Had it really been a year since she had met this man? And then, only a brief time afterwards, married him?

Thomas rose, wrapped his arms around her and kissed her.

"I have a great many reasons to be grateful to Grumpy," he murmured.

Maggie decided she was as besotted with Thomas as she had ever been. Which obviously explained, well, a lot of things.

"And now, let me show you."

He led her to an area where Maggie knew there would be a great many roses in a few months, but few snowdrops. There was a narrow door in the wall that separated the garden from the fields beyond. Maggie had never really paid attention to it. Or wondered what was on the other side. Sheep, most probably.

Thomas took out a key and opened the door. Beyond it was a sizeable plot surrounded by a high stone wall. Cement walks ran between raised beds. In the beds, snowdrops were growing.

Maggie thought she recognised some Green Tears. And some Wasps. And some EA Bowles. And beyond them a dozen plants of Beaumatin's Blonde were flowering. She was pleased to see them. They looked healthy. Vigorous. And after the Beaumatin's Blondes was...

Oh my.

"Someone else who has a good reason to be grateful to you."

It was the Ainswick Orange. A true orange snowdrop with a bright orange ovary and more orange on its inner segments. Unique. And even after its misadventures of the previous year, it had still managed to produce four flowers.

"So you kept it here?"

Maggie had not asked what had happened to the plant after she had brought it to Beaumatin. As the police would have wanted to confiscate it as evidence and she would have had to explain how it had come to be at Beaumatin, she thought it would be better if she did not know exactly.

"It looks like it's doing well," she commented.

Thomas nodded. "Beatrix and I decided it should remain here until a larger clump develops and it can be divided."

"So this is where you keep the most valuable plants?"

"Yes. Once they've left the greenhouse. The door is unremarkable. And it's reasonably secure, unless someone brings a ladder to scale the wall. Which no one would do unless he knew what was behind it."

"Yes. I've hardly noticed the door. And never realised there was anything but a field behind."

"And now we also have Loki and Freya to discourage anyone who becomes too curious."

"And tomorrow is the seminar at Rochford Manor and the tour here."

"Yes."

"May I attend?"

Thomas looked at her sceptically.

"I want to learn…"

He still hesitated.

"Thomas Raynham, isn't my behaviour usually irreproachable, regardless of what I may be feeling personally?"

"It's Thomas. Or Raynham. Just Raynham," he told her for probably the fiftieth time.

"Oh. Right. Well, that's beside the point. You said yourself it would be good for me to experience 'the full show' this year. Seeing as last year there were significant…

51

interruptions, I believe were your words. And Beatrix said I could attend the lectures at the Manor as well. In fact, she thought it was a good idea. And she seems like she could use some help, with Chloe not feeling very well."

Thomas frowned. Finally he said, "Very well. But I'm warning you…"

Maggie cut him off.

"I promise I'll be completely Stepford."

Thomas looked confused.

Maggie linked her arm through his.

"Come. It's lunch time and I have no doubt at all that Mrs Cook has prepared some kind of soup."

Thomas' mouth twitched.

Chapter 8

Sunday, the day before the seminar, Maggie had driven over to Rochford Manor to give Beatrix a large box wrapped in cheerful paper and topped with a bow and to be briefed by David about her duties. She also used it as an opportunity to do some… snooping.

Unlike Beaumatin's more formal gardens, Rochford Manor's snowdrops were naturalised. In season they formed carpets of white under winter-bare trees. On weekends, visitors came by the busload to walk along the paths and exclaim at the display.

Far from the tourist trails was a glade where Rochford's most valuable snowdrops were kept. This was Maggie's destination. She wanted to be absolutely certain that the Beaumatin Blondes she had been assured had been planted in a tidy plot were not there.

Maggie reached the glade and tried to avoid looking at the tree where she had discovered Charlotte. And Emily. She found the location where she had been told the Blondes were planted easily enough. But the snowdrops that she saw blooming were not Beaumatin Blondes, but EA Bowles, a beautiful snowdrop whose six pure white segments formed a graceful parasol.

Maggie searched the rest of the glade on the lookout for the flowers with their distinctive egg-yolk colour. When she did not find them, she sighed with a mixture of regret and relief. So she was right. Someone had taken the snowdrops. And the someone she suspected was Nat Marsh. She felt justified in having contacted Tim and enlisting the help of Crispin.

Now two dozen people were gathered in the Study House at Rochford Manor. They were all strangers to Maggie. Anne, Derek and Damien were attending the seminar the following week.

Based on her experience from the previous year, Maggie had "gifted" Beatrix with a formidable coffee machine. Select the strength you want and the size of your cup. Press a button and beans were freshly ground, water correctly heated and coffee or espresso brewed. There was even a spigot to steam milk for cappuccino, although Maggie had not figured out quite how that worked as yet.

Hot water and a high quality tea bag might produce an acceptable cup of tea, but there was no such thing as an acceptable cup of instant coffee, in Maggie's opinion. So Maggie listened cheerfully to the big beast of a machine grinding beans and filling her cup. A double espresso, please.

Maggie looked around the room. It was a large space painted misty blue with a mural of the Cotswolds in the summer on the wall behind the refreshment table. High-backed wooden chairs surrounded a long refectory table. A laptop was set up on one end of the table, aimed at a projection screen at the far end of the room.

Nat Marsh had not yet arrived. The previous evening, Maggie had gotten an SMS from Crispin to call "on the other number." She did and an excited-sounding Crispin informed her that they believed they had found Marsh's garden. Marsh had paid a visit to several acres of forested land surrounded by a stone wall and spent several hours there.

Maggie had told Crispin the day's schedule and assumed he or Pilchard were tracking Marsh's car. She would keep tabs on him as well during the event. Now that they seemed to have discovered the location of Marsh's garden, she understood that the plan was to check what security measures there were, if any, and to make sure there actually were snowdrops growing there.

"I may not be able to tell a, what was it, Ophelia from a Hippolyta, but I'm sure I'd recognise a snowdrop if I saw one," Crispin had insisted.

So Maggie was to keep Marsh in sight at all times while Crispin and "The Fish," as he called Pilchard, investigated.

The seminar would begin with a talk by David Osborne on the main cultivated snowdrop species—nivalis, elwesii, woronowii, plicatus—and how to distinguish between them. This would be followed by a tour of the Rochford Manor gardens with commentary by both David and Marsh.

After a lunch at the nearby Rochford Inn, the group would travel to Beaumatin, where they would be taken through the gardens by Thomas, again with supporting commentary by David and Marsh. Finally, they would all return to Rochford Manor for a talk by Marsh on "Developing Your Snowdrop Collection," tea and departure.

Maggie watched people serving themselves to tea and—she was pleased to see—coffee, before slowly moving to take their seats. The group reflected what Maggie had discovered to be the typical galanthophile demographic. More women than men by at least two to one and virtually all the men husbands accompanying their wives. Most people were in their mid-sixties. Did one have to be retired to have a proper garden, Maggie wondered. Or perhaps it was that the seminar was being held on a weekday. Finally, everyone was English, i.e., Anglo Saxon. Diversity was not a characteristic of the snowdrop community.

Maggie noticed several people comparing sales sheets of plants they had ordered in advance from Rochford Manor. They could pick up their selection at the end of the day. There would also be plants on display that could be purchased, if a Lapwing or Lord Lieutenant happened to catch an avid collector's eye.

Marsh would also bring some of his own plants to sell. Maggie had learned how Marsh operated. For his rarer, more expensive, varieties, he would have waiting lists. At the beginning of the season, he would fix a price depending on availability and those on the list who were willing, and able, to meet it got a plant on a first come, first served basis. The rarest plants he would auction on eBay, where the sky was the limit.

While Maggie had a certain reluctant respect for the man's unabashedly commercial approach, she had to admit she did find it a bit… crass. And if he were a poacher, there would be no excusing what he did at all.

She had heard quite a few galanthophiles bemoaning the passing of the day of the snowdrop lunch, when collectors would meet over soup and swap varieties among themselves. Accepting money for their little treasures would have been considered far too vulgar. On this basis, Marsh was regarded as being beyond the pale. Still, since he had discovered several varieties and had the reputation for being a prodigious breeder and propagator of the small white flowers, he was grudgingly tolerated by the old guard and was a hero to the newer collectors.

Maggie was helping Beatrix keep a generous supply of cups and saucers on the refreshment table. When everyone had helped himself and found a seat, David called the room to attention. He outlined the schedule for the day and then began his talk.

"What do you do when the label for one of your snowdrops has disappeared and you are having trouble identifying it? Or the label is there but the snowdrop does not look like what you expected? We now have more than one thousand named varieties of Galanthus. Assuming it's not a yellow or one of the Galanthus, which is more easily identifiable like a Wasp or a Diggory, where do you start? Knowing how to tell the differences between the main snowdrop species is a good way to begin.

"And I should warn you now. At the end of my talk, you'll divide up into teams for a test. Like quiz night at your pub. The winning team will receive prizes in addition to glory. So I encourage you to ask questions and take notes."

Halfway through David's talk, Nat Marsh ambled in. He was wearing his usual outfit of baggy corduroy pants, a plaid shirt, a worn blue V-neck sweater, an ancient Barbour jacket and scuffed work boots. His straw-coloured hair still needed a haircut and looked dull. Unwashed. He had the inevitable Highgrove bag slung over his shoulder.

Marsh nodded to Maggie, then walked up and took a seat at the head of the table. The man was certainly not self-effacing, Maggie reflected.

She quietly went outside and called Crispin using the secure phone.

"Your package has arrived. Thanks for sending it," she said.

They had agreed that Maggie would confirm Marsh's arrival at Rochford Manor before Crispin would try to gain entrance to Marsh's secret garden. Although his car was being tracked, this could be the one morning he had lent it to a friend or had car trouble and borrowed a replacement.

"No problem."

"Call you back at lunchtime?"

"Sounds like a plan."

Crispin ended the call and Maggie returned back inside in time to see David dividing his audience into four groups.

"I'm going to show you some slides and you need to identify the species. The team with the most correct answers gets a Rochford Manor Magnet for each member to take home."

Maggie had to admire David's ability to keep his audience engaged.

After the winning team had proudly claimed its trophies, the group was told they could take a brief break before assembling for a tour of the Rochford Manor snowdrops in bloom.

The Rochford Manor gardens were mostly wooded and thousands of snowdrops of various varieties were naturalised beneath the trees. While a frosting of snow from the previous evening meant many of the flowers were not fully opened, the sight was still spectacular.

The tour began and Maggie soon noticed two groups had formed. The largest was surrounding David. They were asking questions about which plants he considered best for beginners, whether different cultivars had different growing requirements, how long it took to get a display like the one they were seeing, whether the varying soil conditions in their own gardens would make a difference.

The second group was smaller. Half a dozen of the attendees had formed a clique around Marsh. They seemed less interested in the Rochford Manor snowdrops than if he thought they had a chance of being able to obtain one of his coveted cultivars. Marsh remained coy.

Good grief, thought Maggie.

Soon it was time for lunch. Twenty-four attendees naturally divided into four tables. Lady Ainswick took one, David took another, Marsh took a third and Beatrix requested that Maggie please take the fourth. Maggie reluctantly agreed.

"As long as they don't ask too many questions about twin-scaling," she told her friend.

Beatrix introduced her to the group as Lady Raynham.

No flinching, she reminded herself.

"And you will be visiting Lady Raynham's gardens at Beaumatin following lunch," Beatrix added.

My gardens? Not hardly, Maggie thought.

Introductions were made. At her table were two women who were members of the same garden club in Peterborough and had come together and two couples. The men were both retired and gave the impression that they had been dragged along by their wives.

Maggie determined where each was on what she was calling the "snowdrop curve"—beginners intrigued by the media hoopla Galanthus were getting, intermediates who were interested in starting a real collection and collectors who wanted the rarest varieties and aspired to be able to name a snowdrop after themselves. Or their cat.

The two ladies from Peterborough were beginners, one of the couples wanted to start collecting and the other couple were obviously disappointed not to be sitting with Marsh but had decided that perhaps Maggie might be useful.

"We're particularly interested in acquiring a Moses Basket," said the man. "Would you happen to have that variety at Beaumatin?"

Maggie congratulated herself on at least knowing the names of all the snowdrops in the gardens.

"No, I'm afraid we don't have any Moses Baskets."

"You specialise in yellows, I understand."

"Yes, although they are still a minority of what is in bloom."

"Will we see Beaumatin's Harriet?" asked the woman, a bit too avidly.

"Yes. It's in the gardens," said Maggie, deciding it was not only Marsh she would need to watch closely.

"Which varieties would you recommend for a beginner," asked one of the women from Peterborough.

"I know Magnet is what is called a 'good doer,' but David Osborne probably knows more about which varieties would do best with your particular growing conditions."

"Will you have snowdrops for sale at Beaumatin?" asked the other wife.

"No," said Maggie and her husband looked relieved.

"But there will be Rochford Manor snowdrops for sale after Nat Marsh's lecture and I believe he has also brought some to sell," she added.

A small bus had appeared to take the group to Beaumatin. David and Nat would go on the bus while Beatrix would go with Maggie in her ancient Land Rover.

"Well, I don't think I embarrassed myself at lunch," said a relieved Maggie.

"My dear, you underestimate yourself. The knowledge you've acquired in the past year is impressive."

"Um. Thank you. Well, I guess you could say I'm immersed so I've been learning by osmosis. Plus I have done some studying. And I am an academic, which helps. I know how to learn things."

"Evidently."

"But I'll be happy to let the experts take over again at Beaumatin. Assuming the bus makes it there."

The bus was proceeding slowly up the single-track lane that led to the estate. Maggie knew tour buses came to Beaumatin quite a few times during the year and were able to navigate the grey road. But apparently the current driver was inexperienced.

Beatrix tsked. She had a schedule to maintain.

"So I'll just tag along and observe. And refer questions to David and Thomas."

"Nat should also be helpful."

"Yes. Nat as well."

Beatrix sensed that Maggie did not care much for Nat. Well, neither did the viscountess as far as that went. However, Maggie had never told Beatrix about her suspicions concerning the man.

The bus finally pulled up in front of the great house and the group descended and gaped like most people did the first time they saw its eccentric mixture of Elizabethan, Jacobean, Georgian and Victorian Gothic architecture.

Thomas came out through an ornate door centred in a Georgian façade. Over the door, the Raynham coat of arms was carved with a motto scrolled underneath. Numquan cede, meaning never give up or never yield. He introduced himself and the visitors set off.

Maggie paused and, out of sight, called Crispin.

"We're at Beaumatin. How was, or is, your visit?"

"I would enjoy telling you about it over a drink. Can we meet?"

Maggie thought. Meeting anywhere in the Cotswolds might be remarked, as she had recently discovered. Even their house in Oxford on Hereford Crescent was not as private as she had assumed.

"I'm having a bit of a week. How about Sunday? My rooms at Merrion. What time would suit you?"

"Between noon and one?"

"Fine. I'll provide a picnic lunch. And leave word with the porter."

Maggie ended the call.

Thomas was explaining how there were other flowering plants that worked well with snowdrops. Cyclamen coum. Aconite. Hellebores. Hamanelis…"

"Hamanelis?" asked one of the women.

"You may know it as witch hazel. Also cornus will still be showing its red. And some are even yellow." He pointed out some specimens.

"Do you have any Green Tears?" asked one of the collectors.

"No. Not at this time," said Thomas smoothly.

"You specialise in yellows," one of the men pointed out. "Do you have an Elizabeth Harrison?"

"No. I believe there is just the single bulb which is being propagated professionally."

Thomas looked for confirmation at David, who nodded.

"Our rarest yellow is our own Beaumatin's Harriet. It is not available to the public as yet."

Thomas led the group over to where a few clumps of the yellow snowdrop were blooming. Several people exclaimed. It was a beautiful flower, Maggie thought.

She watched Nat, who did not seem to be especially interested.

"Will you offer it for sale?" someone asked.

"It has been twin scaled. We hope to have some available in two years. As we do not sell snowdrops at Beaumatin, they will be offered through Rochford Manor."

"Watch this space," said David, smiling.

"What about orange snowdrops? I heard there are orange ones," asked one of the collectors.

At this Nat did appear to be interested. Maggie wondered if Charlotte had told Nick about the Ainswick Orange. And Greenaway would have certainly told Marsh, if her suspicions were correct.

"There is an Anglesey Orange," replied Thomas. "It's under guard at Anglesey Abbey. And also not for sale."

"Didn't I read something about an Ainswick Orange? And some murders? And some bunch of nutters protesting?" asked one of the men.

"Yes. There was an Ainswick Orange. A true orange snowdrop. Sadly it was stolen. Never recovered. However, we are still keeping an cyc out for it in the area around Rochford Manor. So if any of you see it..." said Beatrix smoothly.

The group laughed. Nat looked closely at Beatrix and Thomas, as if to decide whether they were being truthful. And Maggie wondered if anyone in the group would tell the Ainswicks if they saw the rare snowdrop, rather than keep it for himself. One or two perhaps. Galanthomania was certainly tarnishing her view of human nature.

Thomas led them to the greenhouse.

"There is one new snowdrop I can show you today."

He went inside and came out holding a pot.

"This is Beaumatin's Blonde. It is unique in having such significant yellow streaking on the outer segments. It is also being propagated but, in this case, I expect it will be three or four more years before any are on the market."

Maggie watched Nat smirk. He had to have the Beaumatin Blondes that Thomas had given to the Ainswicks. She wondered how he would explain having them to sell. Or perhaps he would offer them privately to collectors he knew who would hide them away in their own gardens. He would certainly be aware of who would be interested.

The others were exclaiming as the pot was passed around.

Nat looked closely through the greenhouse door as Thomas returned the plant. But since Maggie knew that Nick Greenaway had been in the greenhouse several times during his tenure at Rochford Manor, Marsh probably had a good idea of the contents. Thank goodness he didn't know about Beaumatin's own secret garden. She wasn't sure even the Ainswicks knew.

The tour ended. Maggie proposed to Beatrix that they precede the bus this time so they would reach the Manor ahead of the visitors and could put on hot water for tea and make sure the coffee machine was filled with beans.

"An excellent idea," agreed Beatrix.

They arrived well ahead of the bus.

"As Chloe has said she feels well enough today to help with the tea, I wondered if you could assist David with the plant sales. Make sure no one takes a Lapwing or Wasp or Rodmarton or Esther Merton without paying for it."

"Of course."

"And I'll be interested to see what that Nat Marsh has brought to sell. I know you don't think much of him, my dear, and I was also dubious when David proposed asking him to speak. But everyone knows him and having him on the programme is certainly a draw. Commerce. It can be quite distasteful."

Maggie laughed.

Maggie wanted to hear Nat's talk and was glad when she saw that Ian had arrived and was helping David bring out stands full of snowdrops. She took a seat in the back of the room and relaxed with a cup of coffee.

Nat's presentation was about how to develop a snowdrop collection. He had prepared slides with wonderful close-ups of the flowers, which Maggie mentally divided into expensive, more expensive and ludicrously expensive, but which Marsh categorized as best for beginners, launching your collection and perfecting your collection.

And she had to admit that, despite her feelings about the man, he was an excellent speaker. He held the audience's attention and his enthusiasm for his subject was evident. He patiently and thoroughly answered questions and at the end said he had brought some of the snowdrops he had mentioned to sell and also explained how his "special order" and "auction" system worked.

"Given the costs of acquiring an unusual specimen or carrying out a breeding programme, as well as the years it can take to propagate enough plants for the market, I'm sure you understand a seller wants to get the best price possible for a rare Galanthus.

"Auctions achieve that while at the same time are freely open to all. You don't have to be a member of some exclusive inner circle to have a chance of getting one of these cultivars. I know certain people are offended by the auctions, but, well, sticks and stones."

Nat glanced at Maggie when he said that.

"It's not the auctions I find so offensive," she thought. "It's how you acquire the specimens to begin with."

Maggie wondered exactly how much a forensic analysis of the particles of soil inside Marsh's Highgrove bag would cost.

Nat ended his talk with a final slide. It was a large clump of miniature snowdrops. There must have been thirty or forty of the tiny white flowers amid green leaves.

"And here is my latest discovery. I call it 'Gnat,' like the insect. Gnats gather in swarms in season. Like this clump of Galanthus. And of course there's the play on words. I hope to have a specimen or two to offer at auction next season."

"Gnat. An irritating little insect. How appropriate," thought Maggie.

"Where did you find it?" asked one of the women from Peterborough.

"In an old churchyard in Shropshire," said Marsh smoothly.

Maggie went outside to join David. Having noted that no one seemed inclined to pilfer an illicit Esther Merton, she saw that his coterie had again surrounded Nat. It seemed he had also taken some pre-orders and he exchanged flats containing snowdrops for what appeared to be large amounts of cash.

"Impressive," thought Maggie. Perhaps now he could afford to get a proper haircut. She also wondered how much of the cash would be reported to the Inland Revenue.

Marsh had also put out a small table with pots of snowdrops. Several of the group checked out what was on offer, but once they saw the prices, decided a Rochford Manor S Arnot or Colossus or Comet was a better choice.

The attendees drove off, all having purchased quantities of snowdrops.

Beatrix, David, Maggie and Nat stood by the remaining plants.

"Snowdrop locusts," said Maggie.

"Yes. I thought that all went quite well," said Beatrix. "Thank you everyone."

"And a week from today we get to do it again," said David.

"And again on the following Friday," announced Beatrix. "There are already fifteen people signed up who were wait-listed for the first two sessions. And I'm glad you are available, Nat."

Nat nodded.

"And I probably know some people who'd be interested in coming on that Friday as well," he said.

Remembering her mother's adage about "If you can't say something nice, don't say anything at all," Maggie said, "I really enjoyed your talk. I saw quite a few people taking notes. And then when they came out, they referred to them in making their choices."

"It helps when you know what you're talking about."

"Who took your pictures?"

"I did."

"They are quite spectacular."

Nat nodded. Apparently he thought they were good too.

GNAT

"I had better pack up and be off," said Nat.

Oops. And I had better call Crispin, thought Maggie.

SUSAN ALEXANDER

Chapter 9

That night at supper that was, to Maggie's relief, not a pie but a roast chicken, she asked Thomas, "So how do you think the tour went?"

He shrugged. "Since everyone was specifically interested in Galanthus and were not just general gardeners, there were some quite intelligent questions."

"And people were just as interested in your answers," Maggie commented.

Thomas nodded and took a swallow of Saint-Emilion.

"And Beaumatin's Harriet was a hit. As was Beaumatin's Blonde," Maggie added.

"Yes. Beatrix thinks we should get serious about breeding. Propagation. Sales. Since the market seems to be there. I told her I'd think about it."

"Nat gave a really excellent talk when we got back to Rochford Manor. I was surprised. He's quite an engaging speaker. And he had wonderful slides. Close ups of the snowdrops he was talking about. He said he takes them himself."

Thomas looked at Maggie suspiciously, then decided she was being sincere.

"Do you ever take those kinds of pictures? Close ups of your snowdrops?" she asked.

"No. You need the proper camera. Proper lighting. And probably a course in plant photography."

"Do you think I should learn?" Maggie asked.

71

Thomas seemed pleased at the question.

"Would that interest you? It would certainly be useful. If you have the time between being the Weingarten fellow, the Einhorn Foundation director of whatever and best-selling author of controversial publications."

He paused for some more Bordeaux, then noticed Maggie seemed mystified.

"You made the *Times'* list of top non-fiction books this week, if you haven't heard."

"Really? I must admit to having mixed feelings about that. I may even need to develop a new secret identity."

Thomas looked confused.

"It's nothing. I'm joking. But to return to the photography issue, I'll ask David. He would probably know about this kind of thing. Cameras. Courses. Or he'd know someone who'd know."

Thomas stood up and kissed the top of her head.

"I'd like that, Papillon," he said as he helped pull out her chair.

"Refill your glass with your Viognier. There's supposed to be a good programme about Dunkirk on tonight I'd like to watch."

Maggie smiled.

"Oh. I forgot. I need to get some resources from my rooms at Merrion. So I can put together some proposals for the new Global Press book line. And Stanley's lecture series. And Malcolm seems to think I need to produce a new volume as well. Would it be all right if I went Sunday? When we're back from London?"

As soon as she'd said that, her left and right brains piped up.

Right brain. You're asking permission to go to your rooms in Oxford?

Left brain: I know. I know. It just slipped out like that.

R.B.: You really are going Stepford.

L.B.: Tell me.

R.B.: Of course we didn't tell him why we're really going.

L.B.: Being suicidal is a Right Brain kind of thing. Not Left.

Thomas was thinking.

"All right," he said finally in a tone that made Maggie want to hit him.

Instead she asked, "Do you have plans?"

"Just the usual sheep and snowdrops."

"The snowdrops are quite wonderful right now."

"Yes. They are indeed."

Susan Alexander

Chapter 10

The RHS Winter Show was over. Maggie was exhausted from having been helping at the Rochford Manor stand for two days. Snowdrops were selling as quickly as she could take people's money and the rarer, more expensive varieties sold out first. In fact, a fight nearly broke out between two women who reached for the last Deer Slot at the same time.

Thomas had visited the RHS Show but then excused himself, saying he had some business to take care of. Maggie assumed he was meeting about the Raynham real estate holdings with their solicitor, Simon Peevey, who was based in London.

Ian, one of the Beaumatin groundsmen, had also come to the show to help lug the flats of snowdrops in their pots—"in the green"—from the truck to the exhibition hall's storage area and from the storage area to the stand. He was now helping David Osborne disassemble the display. Just as Maggie was saying goodbye, David's mobile sounded.

After a brief conversation, consisting mostly of "Of course," and "All right," and "No, don't be silly, it's fine," from his side, David ended the call and told Maggie, "That was Chloe. She's not doing well and asked if I could come back. I know it means missing the dance, but…"

Chloe was having a difficult pregnancy.

"Of course. We'll miss you, but Chloe should take priority. And there'll be another Snowdrop Ball next year, after all, when you can both come. And I'll let the Ainswicks know."

"Thank you. I'll ride with Ian."

"All right. And if you don't mind, I'll go back to the hotel. I'm going to need a nap if I'm to make it through the evening. I had no idea manning a stand was so tiring."

"Thank you for all your help. And Rochford Manor won an award for our display. That's a big plus. And we've had lots of interest in our seminars. It's good that we were able to schedule a third."

Maggie took a taxi back to the hotel. Thomas was still out. She had just laid down on the bed in her room when the man came in.

"I'm back."

"So I see."

"David and Ian are on their way back to Rochford with the exhibition stand and the few snowdrops that weren't sold. Chloe called. I understand she isn't feeling well."

"All right. I gather the Ainswicks thought David would need to get back for Chloe. I don't think he'll leave an empty place."

He turned to go but Maggie caught his hand.

"Before you go, may I just have an, um, extra moment of Thomas?" she asked.

Thomas looked down at his wife.

"You can have more than just a moment," he smiled and began to take off his jacket.

Afterwards, Maggie managed to nap for an hour. Then she decided she should start getting ready. Whatever that would entail. Thomas had told her she only needed to bring her various "pots," by which she gathered he meant her makeup. He had taken care of everything else, he had said, and looked like "the cat that had swallowed the canary," to use one of her mother's expressions.

However, not being completely trusting when it came to men and their fashion choices, Maggie had given Beatrix the dress she had worn to the ball the previous year to take with her. It was "better to be safe than sorry."

Maggie emerged from her bathroom to find Thomas dressed except for his jacket and a pile of boxes on the bed. And a very long garment bag.

"Thomas?"

"I told you I'd take care of everything."

"Yes, you did, but..."

"I believe we start with these."

He handed her two boxes and watched while she opened them. In the first was a strapless corset of delicate white lace. With garters. The second box held a matching thong barely big enough to cover, well, what it needed to cover.

Maggie glanced at Thomas.

"Go ahead. Please. Put them on."

"What. A reverse strip tease?"

Thomas' mouth twitched.

Maggie slipped on the thong, and then picked up the corset. It hooked up the back.

"Here. Let me help you with that."

Maggie stood still while Thomas slowly fastened the hooks. When he had closed the last one, he put his hands on her shoulders. They felt warm against her cool skin.

He kissed the top of her spine and the side of her neck and murmured, "I can't begin to tell you how much I am looking forward to doing all this in reverse later tonight." And Maggie worried that she was going to melt into a puddle on the carpet.

Thomas handed her the next box. It contained two pairs of translucent stockings so pale they were nearly white. With lacy tops.

"You had better put those on. I'm afraid I'd tear one. And there's an extra pair, just in case."

Maggie carefully pulled on the stockings. Thomas insisted on fastening the garters.

Maggie felt self-conscious. Uneasy. Conflicted. She wasn't used to this kind of thing. Not just having someone else buy her clothes. She felt like a doll that was being dressed up. She knew another woman would go along with it, even enjoy the game. But it wasn't in her nature.

"You really are the staid, reserved Professor Eliot," she told herself.

Thomas picked up a shoebox, and then looked at the garment bag.

"Shoes first? Or dress?"

"That would depend on whether you step into the dress or pull it over your head," said Maggie, trying for practical.

"Hmm. Well, let's do the shoes first then. Just… because," decided Thomas.

The shoes had low heels and were covered with a shimmering, silvery material. They were a perfect fit.

Finally, with a gesture of "ta dah," like a magician pulling a rabbit out of a hat, Thomas unzipped the garment bag.

Maggie stared. It was a fantasy dress, obviously by the same designer as the dress she had worn to the Christmas ball at Beaumatin following the wedding of Thomas' daughter Constance. The dress that Thomas had destroyed. While she had been wearing it.

"Anne helped me find this. Apparently your Neiman's considers you a good customer and they had a record of the, er, other dress. Which was apparently an, um, limited edition. Their lady suggested this one. It's sized just the same as the other one. So the fit should not be a problem."

Maggie reminded herself that she was not a lesser woman, so she nodded and attempted to smile.

"Shall we put it on?"

"All right."

Maggie extended her arms and Thomas slipped the dress on over her head. He carefully zipped the zipper up the back and studied her. Then he turned her so she could see herself in the room's mirror.

The other dress had had delicate, deep green vines embroidered on flesh-toned fabric twining down her arms, her breasts, her back, her thighs, before the tulle flared into a full skirt. That dress was Elfish Princess. This dress was Ice Queen. Flowers and—could it be butterflies? —that looked like they had been transfixed in hoarfrost were woven in a platinum metallic thread over white tulle. Again the dress fit her like a second skin until her thighs, where it flared. The fabric touched the floor in the front and gathered in the back into a short train.

Thomas regarded his wife critically. He had literally torn her old dress to shreds in a blind rage that was a defence against a nearly unbearable hurt. Which he had subsequently discovered was totally unfounded. However, in addition to his fury, he also had to acknowledge that there had been an element of atavistic satisfaction in ripping and shredding the fragile fabric. While Maggie had been wearing it. And he had been...

He imagined doing the same thing again. Maggie. In that dress. Rending the fabric. And... But he had been startled at the cost of the gown and thought perhaps he could find a less expensive alternative if he wanted to relive that sensation.

Maggie stared at her reflection. The dress did fit perfectly. It was just that it was not a dress she would ever have chosen for herself. It was too cold. Beautiful but frigid. Brittle. Remote. She found Thomas icy enough on his own and thought of herself as adding warmth to offset his frostiness. This dress seemed to increase the chill exponentially.

Thomas noticed Maggie's solemn expression.

"What is it, Papillon?"

Maggie gestured. "I'm just rather... overwhelmed."

Thomas assumed he knew what was bothering his wife. When they were first married, Thomas had had to become quite unpleasant before Maggie would agree to accept a household allowance.

"Surely a husband can buy a dress for his wife?"

Maggie still looked troubled.

"And you buy clothes for me," he added reasonably.

Maggie had bought Thomas a sports shirt during a trip to Maine. And a cashmere sweater for Christmas whose colour she had thought matched his eyes. But she could have bought Thomas fifty sweaters for what she assumed this dress had cost.

Repeating to herself like a mantra, "You are not a lesser woman," Maggie took a deep breath. Or as deep a breath as she could in the dress.

"Thank you, Thomas. It's... beautiful."

"Oh. Let me not forget." Thomas turned back to the bed and retrieved the last two boxes.

"This one first," he said.

It was a jeweller's box. Inside was a hair clip. Some silvery metal. White gold? Platinum? Its shape duplicated the shapes of the flowers on the dress. Set into the metal were small diamonds that sparkled.

"You had this made?" Maggie asked.

"I used some diamonds from some old Raynham bijoux that I couldn't recall having been worn in my lifetime. And probably for several generations before that," he explained.

"Here. Let me."

Thomas had become more adept at coaxing Maggie's unruly curls into order than she was herself. He gently pulled them up and fastened them with the clip.

"And finally, there're these."

These were a pair of diamond drop earrings, also in white gold.

"I'll let you put those in and do those final things you women seem to need to do. And I'll finish dressing. We should go down in fifteen minutes or so."

Thomas left and Maggie stood, clutching the box with the earrings. She was afraid to move. Afraid that she'd step on the fabric and tear it. Or catch a heel in the train and fall flat on her face. And if she couldn't even move, just how was she supposed to dance in this dress?

Maggie took a calming breath. She was not a lesser woman. She could do this. She put in the earrings, and then moved stiffly into the bathroom. She needed to adjust her makeup. She swiped some smoky grey eye shadow on her lids and considered blush. Hmm. Maybe not. Ice Queen it was.

Which reminded her. Maggie went and opened the room safe where she had put a small leather case that held her jewellery. She took out a ring. It was a large, ice blue diamond in an art deco setting in which were set a myriad of smaller white diamonds. A woman had given it to her in thanks for having a vicious blackmailer gone from her life.

Maggie had accepted it reluctantly and had never worn the ring. However, it suited the dress perfectly. And again she was trying to expose a villain—she supposed she could call Marsh a villain—so wearing the ring was appropriate both aesthetically and symbolically.

Maggie put on the ring and returned the jewellery case to the safe. Next, she decided she had to practice walking. If she fell, she hoped Thomas would hear the crash and rescue her.

She made it back and forth across the room several times. She tried some simple dance movements. She worried that someone else would step on the short train, even if she managed not to.

Maggie had brought an evening purse of beaded white satin. It would work with the dress. She put in a handkerchief, lipstick, mobile phone, room keycard. Was there anything else she would need? Nothing that would fit in the small bag.

She examined herself in the mirror again. At least her posture was good. Her mother had never permitted her to slouch and made her practice walking on a straight line with a heavy book balanced on her head every day until she had left for college. Now she just had to remember to breath. Not that the dress allowed much room for deep breaths.

Thomas came in, dressed and ready. Oh my. Maggie promptly forgot the breathing thing. She gave a wobbly smile that mimicked what her stomach was doing.

Thomas looked her over one last time, then nodded.

"Come," he said.

Her took her hand and noticed the ring. He raised his eyebrows.

"Legacy," said Maggie.

SUSAN ALEXANDER

Chapter 11

Maggie had attended the Snowdrop Ball the previous year. It had been her first public outing with Thomas. The event, organised by an association of snowdrop breeders, growers, collectors and distributors, attracted everyone who was anyone in the snowdrop world and was usually held after the snowdrop season ended.

This year, it had been decided to schedule the event in conjunction with the Royal Horticultural Society Winter Show, at which most of the breeders and growers, like the Ainswicks, had a stand and which a great many galanthophiles attended. It also meant it was being held in London, which attracted even more people. Then the organisers decided to make the ball white tie, so it was a crowded and glittering anteroom that Maggie entered.

Thomas and the Ainswicks had assembled two tables between them. At Thomas' table were his son James and his wife, Victoria, who lived in London, Simon Peevey, who acted as a solicitor for both Thomas and the Ainswicks, and his fiancé Melanie Carey, Lady Sarah Archibald-Atherton, who was an RHS Vice President and was being escorted by Nat Marsh, and Malcolm Fortescue-Smythe, who was bringing someone designated simply as "and guest."

At the Ainswicks' table were Thomas' son and heir, William, and his wife Gweneth, who was Lord Ainswick's niece, Derek Fiske and Anne Brooks, whose husband Laurence was away at a conference in Brazil. Damien Hawking and a Mrs Mildred Fane, whom Maggie understood was one of Fiske and Hawking's most important clients. The table was completed by Jane and Kenneth March. The Marches had a large retail plant and garden company in

Surrey and were propagating and distributing some of the Rochford Manor snowdrops.

Maggie had been unenthused about Marsh's presence, but in the end decided she would make the best of it. Perhaps she could gather some information that would be useful for Crispin.

After two days at the RHS Show, Maggie saw many people she recognised, even if she could not put a name to each face. Well, that was some progress, she decided. Plus it seemed her normally reclusive husband was making more of an effort to be social. Which was also an interesting development.

The Ainswicks came up to greet them. Beatrix looked at Maggie in her dress.

"My goodness," was her only comment.

Thomas left Maggie with the Ainswicks while he went off to the bar. Gweneth and Anne appeared and Anne examined Maggie's dress.

"I hear you were a co-conspirator," said Maggie.

"Yes. Too bad about the other dress. What happened?"

"An accident," said Maggie vaguely, then added, "And I'll be fortunate to get through the evening without destroying this one as well. A train? What was Thomas thinking?"

"That he wanted to replace your dress. I thought it was very sweet. And it certainly fits perfectly."

"If it fit any more perfectly I wouldn't be able to move. Or breath," said Maggie.

Anne looked around at the crowd.

"Well, this is certainly a grand event. I'm pleased I was invited."

"And your dress is wonderful as well."

Anne was wearing an elegant gown whose top sparkled with silver and blue beading and a sapphire blue chiffon skirt that floated when she moved.

"And you should have a lot of fun with Derek and Damien."

Thomas returned with some white wine for Maggie and whisky for himself. He looked annoyed.

"I just heard from Lady Sarah Archibald-Atherton. Apparently Nat Marsh had some emergency and had to get back to Oxfordshire. She found someone to stand in at the last minute, but she may be somewhat late."

Maggie immediately started to worry about what Marsh's mysterious "emergency" could be. She would have called Crispin, but his mobile was in her room. Maybe she could have her own "emergency" and dash back upstairs and call him.

Thomas was watching her.

"Maggie. A word," he said and led her off to a quieter place at the side of the room.

"What is it?" he demanded.

"Nothing. I just remembered…" she began evasively while thinking that the ball would be a perfect opportunity for Marsh to go poaching, while the whole galanthophile community was in London and away from their gardens.

Were Beaumatin or Rochford Manor being targeted? She should call Mrs Cook and tell her to make sure Loki and Freya were on patrol. And David Osborne....

"Maggie, are you off on your crusade against Nat Marsh again? I thought you said you were giving that up. I want to enjoy tonight, not be saddled with some pig-headed crackpot..."

"I am not..." she began angrily. Then took a deep breath. Or as deep a breath as she could in her dress. All right. If Thomas wanted Stepford, he'd get Stepford.

"Very well, my lord. I promise you will enjoy yourself," she murmured. She reached up and gave him a kiss on his cheek. Then, before he could react, Maggie started off to where she saw Thomas' sons and their wives, who were talking to the Ainswicks.

Thomas watched his wife walk away. He didn't believe her for an instant. And felt a fleeting urge to dispatch this dress the same way he had the last. Well, the night was young. He'd see how it went.

"Glitter and be gay, that's the game I play," Maggie said to herself, remembering the song from *Candide*. She wondered if Derek knew it. He certainly had a fondness for show tunes. She would have to ask him, Maggie decided as she rejoined her friends and family. She guessed she could think of William, Gweneth, James and Victoria as family. Sort of.

Gweneth, a pretty blonde, exclaimed over Maggie's dress. "I thought you'd wear the one you did at Constance's wedding," she said.

Maggie glanced at William, who looked like a younger version of his father, and knew what had happened.

At least to the dress if not the exact circumstances. Apparently the man did not share confidences with his wife. Maggie sent him a look that said, "Thanks."

"There was an accident. A pity."

Maggie caught a whiff of citrusy spicy aftershave and realised Thomas had rejoined the group.

"Another glass of wine?" he asked and took her empty glass.

"Please," she said.

Maggie saw Malcolm Fortescue-Smythe approaching with a woman on his arm at least three decades younger than the publisher. Tall and blonde, she wore a tight black dress with a slit in its skirt that showed off long legs that were an easy match for Maggie's.

Malcolm stared at Maggie for a long moment, and then introduced her as "Lady Raynham" to his companion. Maggie tried not to cringe. She had figured on being Lady Raynham-ed tonight, but after the book launch, she had become used to being Professor Eliot again.

"And this is Tatiana," he said.

Hmm. Gorgeous. Flawless, in fact. Mono-named. Model probably, Maggie decided. She introduced Malcolm and "Tatiana" to the others. The woman had a heavy accent. Czech? Slovak? Eastern European certainly. Maggie decided the woman's language skills were probably not of great importance. At least not to Fortescue-Smythe. Possibly he got enough vocabulary at work.

Gweneth and Anne exchanged glances.

Derek was entertaining his friends with a review of a musical he and Damien had seen the previous evening, complete with snippets of the songs. He gave it a thumbs down.

Maggie decided she would go to the Ladies' Room before the dinner started and make some calls from there, out of earshot of Thomas. She murmured her destination to her husband.

Thomas pulled her aside and said, "Before you go, my tie feels like it's askew. Or loose. Could you fix it, please?"

He took her purse and wine glass so both her hands were free.

Maggie made the most minor of adjustments.

"There. You are once again the pinnacle of sartorial perfection," she smiled.

She reached for her purse.

"I'll hold this while you, er, freshen up. I assume you may need both hands to manage your dress," he said mildly.

Maggie wasn't fooled for an instant about Thomas' motives, but she didn't bat an eye.

"Thank you. That's very kind. I won't be long."

When Maggie returned, the crowd was slowly making its way into the ballroom.

Thomas led Maggie to their table—apparently he had checked its location in advance. It was round and she was pleased to find she was actually sitting next to her husband rather than at the opposite end of a long table as she did at Beaumatin when they had guests. Or was she pleased?

Thomas seemed less like a husband and more like a watchdog at the moment. Which reminded her of Loki and Freya. She hoped they were on guard.

While she had been away, Simon Peevey had arrived. Simon was a solicitor who specialised in estates and trusts. With his white-blonde hair, he looked like a cross between Boris Johnson and the Michelin tire man, but Maggie had seen him throw a punch and knew he was no wimp.

According to Anne, Simon had been engaged to Melanie, a pretty brunette, for three years. Melanie lived with her invalid mother and her mother's two unmarried sisters in a brick Victorian house in Primrose Hill across the street from Simon, who also lived with his widowed mother.

"Romeo and Juliet had an easier time getting married than Simon and Melanie," was Anne's comment. "And it's not even like their families disapprove. Sometimes I want to knock their heads together and say get married and get on with it. But no one's asked for my advice. As usual."

Malcolm Fortescue-Smythe was sitting on Maggie's left and was telling Maggie about the most recent figures from her book sales, which were even better than his most optimistic projections.

"Your work has obviously hit a nerve," he concluded.

Meanwhile, James was manfully trying to converse with Tatiana, who was smiling and nodding without convincing anyone that she understood very much.

"Malcolm, what were you thinking?" was Maggie's reaction.

Maggie noticed Thomas was standing. The RHS officer must have finally arrived. She looked up and nearly dropped her wine glass when she saw Crispin escorting a formidable-looking matron in her seventies. The other men stood.

Crispin's eyes widened when he saw Maggie. Then he grinned ruefully and shrugged.

Thomas introduced Lady Sarah Archibald-Atherton to the table.

"And this is my nephew, Lennox," she said.

"Not Crispin after all. Why am I not surprised," thought Maggie. Crispin/Lennox was avoiding making eye contact.

Maggie wondered if Crispin actually were Lady Sarah's nephew. The grey-haired woman in a vintage dress of deep blue lace didn't look like someone who would participate in something deceptive. But who knew. Who even knew if she really were Lady Sarah Archibald-Atherton, although Thomas seemed to know her, as did Fortescue-Smythe? And Crispin, no, Lennox was looking extremely fine in his white tie and tails.

Introductions finished, Crispin pulled out Lady Sarah's chair and the men sat.

Suddenly Maggie felt like it was all just too much and decided she would pretend that she did not know any of these people, Thomas included, and just listen attentively and make polite rejoinders when required. As though she were at a conference dinner. Tatiana wasn't the only one who knew how to nod and smile.

She would also try to alert Crispin about Marsh. Although what he could do while he was here was another matter. Maggie assumed he must know he was Marsh's stand-in. But perhaps not.

Dinner was served and Maggie was relieved to see the starter was not potted shrimp, but a salmon tartare. She left the main course, which was some sort of elaborately prepared veal chop, and was amused to notice Tatiana did the same. Maggie did have more of the white wine, which was very pleasant, she had decided.

Tables were being cleared and a small orchestra was setting up. Maggie wanted to go to the Ladies' Room and realised Thomas still had her purse. Somewhere. She could see no sign of it.

She murmured her excuses to Thomas and left. Tatiana followed her.

"Nice dress," managed the model. Maggie guessed she could not be much more than twenty-one or twenty-two. Good grief, Malcolm, she thought.

"Thank you," Maggie smiled.

"You know Mal-come?"

"Yes. His company publishes the books I write." Maggie said and hoped her vocabulary was simple enough.

"You write books?" asked Tatiana, intrigued.

Maggie nodded. She wondered what kind of books the woman would think she wrote. Probably not what in fact she did write.

Then she rebuked herself. The woman might have a PhD in biogenetics. No, biogeneticists knew English. Slavic literature, then. And she certainly knew less Czech than this stunning creature knew English.

But had it really been fair of Malcolm to drag the woman to such an event? Full of sexagenarian gardening types? She even felt alien here. She couldn't imagine what Tatiana must be feeling.

"Now we dance," Tatiana said. She looked unhappy.

"Don't you like to dance?" Maggie asked.

"Rock and roll okay. But not fancy stuff," Tatiana admitted.

Maggie laughed. "Me too."

The women returned to their table, Maggie with much more sympathy for the model than before.

The orchestra had begun to play. As Maggie had feared, the repertoire was pre-Beatles. And pre-Elvis. Probably even pre-Andrews Sisters.

Maggie was not a good dancer. Or not when it came to "ballroom" dancing. She was hopeless at following her partner's lead and her tendency to be clumsy exacerbated the problem. Unfortunately, Thomas was an excellent dancer and liked to waltz. And fox trot. And quickstep. Thank goodness he didn't like to tango. She had once suggested to Thomas that when he danced with her he should wear steel-toed boots like a construction worker rather than the elegant pumps that accessorised his formal wear. He was not amused.

The orchestra finished one number and prepared to begin another. Thomas didn't even ask, he simply took her hand and said, "Come."

Maggie followed obediently. Did the Stepford Wives dance?

Maggie had developed a coping mechanism she called her "out of body" technique. When in Thomas' arms, she simply let her mind go blank. She seemed better able to follow him that way. He just had to choose between witty banter and her being an adequate partner. She could not do both at the same time.

The orchestra was playing a Cole Porter tune. "Why Can't You Behave?"

Thomas murmured, "How appropriate. They're playing your song."

Maggie gave him a look and then went back into what Thomas called "Eliotshire." Well, at least she no longer stepped on his toes.

Maggie danced with Simon and William and Damien.

Malcolm asked her next.

As he took her in his arms, he said, "Well, who knew that beneath the Clark Kent of staid, reserved Professor Eliot there lurked Lady Raynham, Superman. Or perhaps Wonder Woman would be more accurate."

Maggie sighed. "In fact, I tend to think of it as being the other way around."

"Really?" The publisher was surprised. "I would think this would be much more fun. In fact, were you not already married, I might begin to rethink my decision to remain a bachelor."

Maggie knew Malcolm had been married once when he was young. The divorce had been ugly and left him with no desire to repeat the experience.

"Ah, but if I were not married, I would still be staid, reserved Professor Eliot," she reminded him.

"Yes. Like the heroine in some old time movie, hiding her beauty behind a severe hairstyle and unflattering eyeglasses, until the hero sees what's really there. Sleeping Beauty for the modern age."

Maggie was taken aback. Was the man flirting or just being gallant to one of his authors?

Then she noticed that Thomas was dancing with Tatiana. They were doing what Maggie referred to as the high school prom shuffle. Neither looked very happy. She smiled to herself.

"Speaking of staid, I'm surprised to see you at our event. I would assume this is not your usual sort of thing."

"I read about the craze for snowdrops and was curious. Thomas asked if I'd like to come and I accepted. I even wondered if there might be an interesting book…"

"I'm not sure Galanthomania would fit in well with climate change and peak oil," Maggie pointed out, referring to his publishing house's usual subjects for its more popular volumes.

"You're right of course. Still, it's an interesting phenomenon. Galanthomania."

The dance ended.

"Well, enough intelligent, even amusing, conversation," he remarked.

Maggie looked at him quizzically.

"I know. I know. Tatiana gives new meaning to the term 'arm candy.'"

Maggie was tempted to make a remark about that was the risk of being a professional bachelor, but decided she shouldn't kick a guy when he was down.

She turned and found Crispin standing in front of her.

"May I have this dance?" he asked and Maggie could tell he was trying not to laugh.

She nodded. Coolly.

The orchestra began to play a waltz and he whirled off with her.

"So, Crispin…." Maggie said.

"So, Lady Raynham," he replied.

"Yes, but you already knew that. From Tim's famous files."

"Certainly. But there was no indication that Lady Raynham looked like this."

He widened the space between them, indicated her dress, and then pulled her closer again.

Maggie gritted her teeth.

"Are you really Lennox Archibald-Atherton? And is Lady Sarah actually your aunt?"

"Yes. For my sins."

"Did you know you're replacing Nat Marsh? He was supposed to be here, but he cancelled at the last minute."

They were near the bar. Crispin paused.

"Would you like a drink? And we can talk?"

"Please."

When Crispin returned with some white wine for Maggie and some whisky for himself, he asked, "Shall we find someplace more private?"

Maggie noticed Thomas watching them from across the room. She smiled in his direction. If he saw her go off with Crispin, she was fairly sure her Ice Queen dress would meet the same fate as her previous one. And she really wanted to avoid that.

"No. Let's stay here. Going off would be a bit obvious and Thomas…"

Crispin also noticed Thomas watching them. He raised his glass and nodded to the peer, who returned to a conversation he was having with Anne.

"He's already unhappy about what he considers to be my fixation on Marsh."

"Fixation?"

"He thinks I'm obsessed. But please, believe me, if it turns out I'm just being fanciful, I will be quite relieved. However, to get back to Marsh, I'm worried that he cancelled his appearance here so he could to go snowdrop poaching."

Crispin nodded. "I haven't had the chance to tell you. We were able to put a tracking device on Marsh's car. He's in Warwickshire. In someone's garden. Name of Epsley. The Fish is following him."

"The Fish?"

"Fred Pilchard. The colleague I mentioned? We call him The Fish."

Good grief. Maggie wondered if The Fish possessed superpowers. Like being able to breath under water.

"Anyway we'll have a better idea of what Marsh is up to if any thefts are reported."

Maggie nodded.

"Do you know if these people, the Epsleys, are here?"

"No. But we can check the list of attendees."

"And I'm going to check out Marsh's secret garden tomorrow. I'll let you know what I find when we meet on Sunday."

Crispin took Maggie's glass, put it back on the bar, and swept her back onto the dance floor. Crispin was also a good dancer and she had to admit she enjoyed the sensation of, well, being in his arms.

"Don't even think such things, Eliot," she reproved herself. And God forbid Thomas should get the same idea.

Crispin requested a second dance.

"Purely for pleasure this time. Not business," he explained.

Afterwards, he returned her to Thomas and then asked Victoria to dance. She looked pleased at the invitation.

Thomas looked at her.

He didn't even need to ask.

"Archibald-Atherton provided me with some much appreciated refreshment. And it seems we have some common acquaintances. In Oxford."

Thomas nodded. "His father and I were at Balliol together. Although I believe Lennox defied family tradition and attended Magdalene. Lady Sarah tells me he's now a rising star in one of the ministries."

The Ministry of Cloak and Dagger, Maggie said to herself. She smiled at Thomas.

"Another dance, Papillon? I am inclined to be appreciative, having just experienced someone who is even less adept than you."

"Tatiana?"

"Um. And no conversation either. Poor Malcolm."

"I think Malcolm knew exactly the bargain he was making. And I am sure she would be much better with Jay Zee. Or Shakira. Or Lady Gaga. We discussed it. Apparently we have that in common."

"And don't forget your legs," Thomas murmured as he danced away with her.

Chapter 12

They were back upstairs in their room. Or rooms, Maggie reminded herself. Thomas had booked a suite and an adjoining bedchamber.

Thomas' face was unreadable as he handed Maggie back her purse.

"So I gather Loki and Freya had a quiet night. And apparently there were no calls for help from Rochford Manor either," he said pointedly.

Maggie mentally bit her lip to keep herself from telling him that the Epsleys from Warwickshire were probably not so lucky.

"And Cedric commented on how much your dancing had improved since the previous year. And even though Anne berated me about getting you a dress with a train—apparently she had failed to notice this detail previously--I see that no damage seems to have occurred. And Beatrix as usual hoped I was adequately appreciative of your many virtues. Although I am not sure I was as appreciative as Malcolm. Or young Archibald-Atherton…"

All right. Maggie decided she was done with being Stepford.

"Do you have any idea how completely insufferable you can be?" she demanded.

"Yes. A very good one. As it is the result of centuries of breeding and a great many opportunities to practice," he replied, unperturbed.

"Errrgh!"

Maggie turned and started to walk towards her room.

Thomas quickly caught up with her and grabbed her arm.

"No. Stand still."

With his free hand he gently removed her hair clip and ran his fingers through her curls. His grip on her arm tightened and he was surprised to feel her trembling.

"Don't worry, my dear. I won't say I'm not tempted. In fact, I am extremely tempted. But your gown is in no danger. Or at least not tonight."

And he very slowly started to pull the zipper down the back of her dress.

Chapter 13

Maggie had stopped to shop for lunch before arriving at her rooms at Merrion. Some good cheeses. Some good bread. Some charcuterie—she assumed Crispin ate meat. Some fruit. Some Bordeaux she had received as a gift that she thought looked promising, it just needed to be opened some minutes before serving to "breathe." The Viognier she already knew and enjoyed. She liked its name as well. It was called Verité. Truth.

She had plates, cutlery, glasses, napkins. She was ready.

Maggie had not been in her rooms since the end of the Michaelmas term. They seemed stuffy, despite the scout's coming in to clean. Although the day was chilly, she threw open a window.

There was still time. A lot of time if Crispin arrived closer to one than noon. And what she had told Thomas about needing some materials for the new roles she was undertaking was not a total fabrication.

So she went through her bookshelves, took some journals, papers and other volumes she thought would be helpful, and put them in her briefcase. There. Done.

There was a soft knocking at her door.

"Come in."

It was Crispin. Early. He was wearing an ancient Burberry. Under the Burberry, he had on brown corduroy pants, a tweed jacket, a tan sweater vest, a yellow shirt and a bow tie.

Maggie stared, then laughed.

"You've got the clothes right. But no one would ever mistake you for a Don. Your hair is all wrong. There's too much of it. The required look is thinning. If not actually balding. And your eyes. No Oxford Don would ever have those eyes."

Those eyes glinted and Maggie took a step back.

"What are you saying, Eliot?" she scolded herself.

"Anyhow, please, come in. Um, may I take your coat?"

Crispin removed his coat and handed it to Maggie. He looked around the room, with its refectory table and wooden chairs, leather armchairs, solid desk and bookshelves. Then he studied her in her grey cashmere turtleneck and matching wool slacks.

"You seem to be doing Oxford Don well enough for both of us. I think I prefer the Ice Queen. Although I understand best-selling author is another option. What would she look like, I wonder."

"Oh dear. That. Yes. Not something I ever really aspired to," Maggie said ruefully.

"No? I thought everyone wants to write a best seller. Just like everyone secretly wants to be a rock star. Why Guitar Hero sells so well."

Maggie laughed and shook her head.

"Anyhow, I promised you a picnic. So picnic it is. I hope you like Haut Brion."

Crispin examined the bottle. Looked impressed. He poured some into a glass, swirled it around. Held it up to the light.

"It has legs. Rather like you," he remarked.

He toasted her and took a sip.

"Very nice. From the Beaumatin cellars? I'm sure they're impressive."

"No. Although they are. This was a gift from a colleague."

"Well, thank you. You're having white, I assume?"

He opened the Viognier, filled a glass for Maggie and added more to his own.

"Shall I get my report out of the way and then we can enjoy our picnic?" he asked.

"As you wish," Maggie said. She indicated the armchairs and they sat down.

Crispin was about to start when her mobile sounded. Her current ringtone was the Eagles' "All She Wants to do is Dance."

Crispin heard it, looked surprised, then grinned.

Maggie was going to refuse the call when she noticed the caller ID. It was Thomas.

"Please excuse me. I need to take this," she said.

"Hello?" She walked into the adjoining room.

"Hi. I arrived without event and am going through, um, things. How are the sheep?"

The sheep were fine. The snowdrops as well. He was calling to ask if she could drop by the house on Hereford Crescent and pick up a jacket he wanted from Mrs Royce, the housekeeper there. He had already called the woman. She'd have it ready.

Crispin had gotten up and was examining her book collection. He pulled a volume off a shelf, which caused a chain reaction that ended with several other volumes crashing to the floor.

There was silence on the other end of the mobile. Then, "Is someone there?"

"A student. Or I guess now it's a former student. He saw I was here and asked if he could borrow one of my books. On the Irish Diaspora. I told him to help himself. I guess I should have gotten it for him," she said easily.

"It sounds like you had better go help him."

"I will. Take care, Thomas."

"You too, Papillon."

Maggie ended the call.

Errrgh. She hated lying to Thomas. She might as well be having an affair. Well she guessed in a way she was. Just not a love affair. But it was certainly clandestine.

"Sorry about that. Was that his lordship?"

Maggie nodded. She sat down again.

"You were about to tell me…"

"Oh yes. So we have been in the dragon's lair. The monster's den. Possibly even the gnat's nest. Whatever you'd choose to call it."

"Was there security?"

"Your Mr Marsh had a fake security camera glued to a gatepost. Plastic. It displayed a red blinking light that ran off a battery. It wouldn't have fooled your average five year old."

Maggie smiled.

"So no Rottweilers? Laser alarms? Retinal scanners? Motion detectors?"

"Nothing. It was almost disappointing. Hardly a good use of my skills."

"Did you see any snowdrops?"

"Yes. Small white flowers by the hundreds. They started around four hundred yards in."

Maggie sighed.

"Well, thank you. Very much."

She stood.

"I guess it's true what they say about not paying attention to rumours. I'm sure I'll be fine."

Crispin reached out, grabbed a wrist, twisted her arm up behind her back and pulled her into his lap. She was immobilized and it had only taken a second.

Maggie was afraid that if she moved, her shoulder would be dislocated.

"Ouch! Crispin!"

Deep green eyes looked into hard blue ones. Which were also looking... dangerous. Maggie wondered exactly what other kinds of work Crispin did for Tim.

"Those woods had an ugly feel about them. And I am not an imaginative man. Well, at least not about those sorts of things. So you are going to promise me, Margaret Spence Eliot, that you will not go in there without me. Word of honour. Cross your heart and hope to die. And remember, I'll know if you're lying and it will not end well for you."

Maggie glared.

Crispin pulled her arm up fractionally higher.

"Ow! Crispin!"

"Promise."

"All right. All right. I promise. Now please."

Crispin looked into her eyes and decided he believed her. Her eyes that were so impossibly green. He leaned forward and kissed her.

It was not a kiss on the cheek. Or a collegial kiss. Or a kiss one would get from a father or brother or uncle. It was a real kiss, passionate and hungry.

Maggie was so shocked that at first she did not react. Plus she still had fears for her shoulder. Then, when she did react, she realised she was not feeling outrage, but pleasure. She was enjoying Crispin's kiss.

Oh dear. This was bad. And Crispin was, um, excellent at what he was doing.

Crispin paused to catch his breath. He noticed Maggie's dazed expression.

"Don't worry, Moppet," he said and ruffled her curls. He set her back on her feet and stood.

"Now how about that picnic? And there's more you should know."

Maggie rubbed her aching shoulder. She was speechless. But Crispin was sitting down at the table and regarding the feast appreciatively. He had moved on. Well, then, so would she.

"Stay cool, Eliot," she told herself.

Maggie sat down across from him. He refilled both of their glasses and took some bread and cheese and ham.

"So what else should I know?"

"A theft was reported. The Epsleys returned from that affair in London to find someone had entered their garden and stolen all their most valuable snowdrops. Just dug them up in the night. It's a sizeable property, with no close neighbours and no live-in help, so there was no one to notice anything. The house has a security alarm system, but not the grounds. I got a list of the missing plants. And noticed there seemed to be a bed of freshly planted snowdrops at Marsh's place. But you'd need to tell me if they are the same varieties."

Maggie nodded.

"And we found out who owns the land Marsh is using. Or who holds the title. It's a Mrs Gertrude Jenkins. Turns out it's his maternal grandmother. She died thirty years ago but the deed was never transferred. Although it's Marsh's legally. He inherited it. But no one would ever have found it if all that were done was a property search in his name."

Crispin helped himself to more food. Maggie drank some wine. She was still a bit stunned by what had happened. Not that she had been kissed. Men had kissed her before. But by her reaction. Bad Maggie, she rebuked herself again. But as Crispin seemed to have forgotten about it, then so would she. Obviously it was a guy thing and she shouldn't take it seriously.

"Tell me. How did someone go from Magdalene to working with our Tim?"

How did you..."

"Don't worry. Tim hasn't sent me your file. Although turnaround would be fair play. Thomas went to Balliol with your father."

Crispin grimaced.

"And my question remains."

"Long story short. I was engaged to be married after I graduated Magdalene. She ran off with my best friend instead. I licked my wounds by joining the army. You can imagine what Father's reaction to that was. It was bad enough that I hadn't gone to Balliol. I made it into the SAS. The wounds healed. I got tired of the Nearer East. And foreign climes generally. But apparently my conduct had been meritorious enough so the prodigal son was forgiven, a fatted calf was killed and Father introduced me to a certain member of his old boys' network. It turned out Tim was looking for a fellow with my, um, skillset..."

"And what exactly is your skillset?" Maggie asked.

Crispin's hard blue eyes grew even harder.

"Nothing I can, or want to, talk about."

"Oh."

"Let's just say there are niches in Tim's department for an Oxford grad with a Special Forces background."

"Fair enough."

"And you? How did you go from being Professor Margaret Spence Eliot," he gestured at the room, "to Lady Raynham, second wife of the twenty-eighth Baron?"

"That wasn't in the file?"

"Just the fact of it. Not the story behind."

"Oh. Well. I was on a sabbatical year and I had a book to write and I got writer's block. My friend Anne… you may have met her at the ball. She's the wife of a colleague and one of the people who'll be keeping an eye on Marsh at tomorrow's seminar. She arranged for me to use a picturesque cottage in a quainter-than-I-you-die village in the Cotswolds."

Crispin made a face.

"It was supposed to be a distraction-free environment. It was. But even that didn't help. So next she decided I needed a break and she dragged me off to a snowdrop weekend at Rochford Manor. It included a tour of Thomas' gardens."

"And two murders."

"Yes, I suppose that would be in the file. Anyway, that's how I met Thomas and after that, well, things seemed to happen quite quickly."

"Dazzled by the title and the estate?" said Crispin cynically.

"Why does everyone think that?" Maggie was indignant.

"I have a perfectly good title of my own. For which I worked very hard. And if I were never called Lady Raynham again, it would be fine with me. Although probably not with Thomas. I certainly don't need money and Beaumatin is like living in a museum. There are portraits of the barons—and their wives and children and dogs and horses—hanging everywhere. Thank goodness they're not the kind that follow you with their eyes. The attic alone could fill the V&A with eight hundred years of antiques. There's even a Constable hanging above the drawing room fireplace…"

"Having regrets?"

"Regrets? No, not really. No."

"So why did you marry his lordship?"

"Well, for the usual reasons I suppose."

"In my experience, the reasons people marry vary as much as their marriages themselves."

"Have you ever been married?"

"Me? Good God, no."

"Oh. Well." Maggie decided she was not going to talk about her feelings for Thomas.

"Anyway, it's not like I wanted to get married. That was all Thomas' idea. My attitude towards marriage, well, I guess you could say I've always been highly ambivalent. At best. And I'm still, um, adjusting."

Crispin was studying her closely.

"Anyhow. Does that fill in the blank?"

"For now."

"And are you sure, since it seems like it's only a question of trespassing, not disabling hi-tech security systems or fighting off Dobermans that you really need to come with me? I am sure Lady Raynham of Beaumatin would never be prosecuted for climbing over a wall to explore a snowdrop wood. Or even Professor Eliot. And I'm sure Tim—and the nation—can find better things for you to do."

Crispin leaned across the table and grasped her wrist. Hard.

"You made a promise, remember? I'm holding you to that."

"All right."

"It's a bad place, that wood."

"All right."

"And your file also includes the fact that you're an accomplished liar and can look at a man with your deep green eyes and not even blink while you're bamboozling him."

"That's…"

"And that certain of your performances could have swept the BAFTAs, the Oscars and the Screen Actors' Guild awards."

"Humpf."

"So I need to know I can trust you."

"I made a promise. I am not in the habit of breaking promises. I was just asking, is all. Of course you can trust me."

They both became aware that he was still holding her wrist. He released it and leaned back.

"And you've also shot people."

"They were bad people. About to do worse things. And I'm a good shot. Nobody died."

"Yes. It says that too."

"And that's why we got Loki and Freya."

"Who?"

"Our Tibetan mastiffs. So I wouldn't need to shoot people."

"And how is that working out for you?"

"So far, so good."

"Glad to hear it."

They smiled at each other.

"And I assume you don't even need a gun. Special Forces and all."

"Thirty ways to dispatch a man with my bare hands."

Maggie decided she was not going to ask how many of those ways he had used in the past and if any had been after he had started working for Tim.

"Good to know."

Crispin poured himself another glass of wine. Maggie hoped he wasn't driving.

"Grapes? Clementines?" She indicated the fruit.

"Only if you peel the grapes and feed them to me while I'm lying with my head in your lap."

"Sorry. I don't do the grape peeling thing."

"I'd settle for skin on if the remaining criteria were met."

Maggie decided this was just witty banter, Crispin-style.

"So we're agreed. Tomorrow, while the seminar is being held and we can be sure Marsh is at Rochford Manor, we'll go and I'll take a look at those snowdrops."

"You wouldn't consider letting me go alone with a camera?"

"No. Although if you wanted to bring along a camera that would be helpful."

"And a copy of the *Daily Post* so we can do a proof-of-life?"

"Actually, that's not a bad idea."

Crispin shook his head.

"I know. Thomas tells me I'm pig-headed."

"Well, he's right about that."

"Thank you!"

Crispin grinned. He stood.

"Thank you for the picnic, but now I must be off. Super villains to defeat. Worlds to save."

"I know I'm supposed to think you're being silly, but I'm more than half convinced that's exactly what you do. Do."

"I just hope Marsh is no super villain. I've been in a lot of bad places and those woods felt like one of them."

Maggie had walked with Crispin to the door. Suddenly he turned, grabbed her and kissed her.

Oh dear, thought Maggie. If the kiss were an exam, Crispin would definitely get a first.

Crispin finished and released her.

"Sorry. Couldn't help myself."

He left.

Maggie picked up Thomas' jacket from Hereford Crescent and drove back to Beaumatin.

She thought about Crispin. Yes, he was certainly attractive. Extremely attractive. And he definitely fell into the category of being mad, bad and dangerous to know. And she could not deny she had enjoyed being kissed by him.

Then she wondered if kissing were a skill taught in a Special Forces course. When the seduction of an enemy was required. Along with thirty ways to kill someone barehanded.

So Crispin was a good, no, make that great, kisser. But beyond that? She was certain she had none of the feelings for him that she had for Thomas. Crispin's blue eyes did not make her feel like she was in danger of melting into a large puddle on the floor. Her stomach did not go wobbly at the sight of him. Like it had with Thomas from virtually the moment they had met. And Crispin certainly did not make her feel like she had come home, like she did when Thomas held her.

And if the next day were the last time she saw Crispin. Which she expected that it would be. Well, it would not be like her whole world had suddenly fallen into bottomless darkness, like it had those times when she had thought she had lost Thomas.

She loved Thomas. Besottedly. Beyond reason. And whatever feelings she had for Crispin... Well, they were not love. In that sense. She had no doubt. No doubt at all. She would just have to be careful not to let Crispin kiss her again. Assuming he would even want to.

SUSAN ALEXANDER

Chapter 14

Maggie arrived back at Beaumatin in time to join Thomas for a cocktail. Or an aperitif, in her world. Since she nearly always had white wine, she was not sure the term cocktail applied.

"Did you find what you needed?"

"Yes. Or most bits."

"And the student. Did he find that book?"

"On the Irish Diaspora? Yes, but only after a determined search. One of these days I must really reorganize my library. It was just luck it wasn't at Hereford Crescent. Or here."

"Maybe you could make your own digital catalogue. Like you did for our plants here."

"I could, of course. But that would mean every time I took a book or journal home with me from Merrion, or brought one back, I'd have to record it. And I'm not sure I have the discipline. And if I didn't do that, it would mean the database would soon be completely worthless. At least for using it to know where a particular volume was. The good thing about plants is they normally stay put once they're in the ground.

"And besides, it's good for me to try to remember where things are. It's a kind of senility test. Isn't short term memory the first thing to go if you're getting Alzheimer's?"

Thomas looked taken aback.

"And what are your, er, test scores?"

"So far, so good," Maggie smiled.

"A first, then," said Thomas, sounding relieved.

Mrs Cook announced that supper was ready. They went into the dining room where Maggie found that the housekeeper had prepared a salad and, what a surprise, shepherd's pie.

Maggie had some salad while Thomas concentrated on the pie.

Thomas nattered on about how Beaumatin's snowdrops were doing. Maggie listened attentively and asked questions.

Suddenly Thomas stopped.

"Thomas?"

"Um…"

"What is it?"

"My dear, you are being much too amenable."

"Amenable?"

"Yes. Saint Margaret the Amenable. It makes me… suspicious."

"Because I'm taking an interest in snowdrops? I'm trying to accelerate my progress up what for me is a rather steep learning curve. I thought I was supposed to be interested in snowdrops, Not that I'm only doing it out of a sense of duty. I'm finding I quite like snowdrops.

"And what is this? Damned if I do and damned if I don't? I thought you preferred… amenable. You tend to get cranky when I do things you don't agree with. Or approve of."

Maggie was indignant.

"I don't want feigned docility."

"Feigned?"

"It's not like I don't know you. You could give Loki lessons in tenaciousness."

"Pig-headedness, you mean."

"Yes. All right. Pig headedness." Thomas said through clenched teeth.

"Well, it's certainly been fortunate for you that I'm... pig-headed."

Thomas had to concede Maggie had a point.

"Are you attending the seminar at Rochford Manor again on Monday?"

"Why?"

"So you can keep watch on Marsh?"

Maggie threw up her hands.

"So this is about Marsh? No. I'm not. David gave me some recommendations on digital cameras that were good for taking botanical pictures. Close ups of flowers. Apparently you need really good depth of field. And a particular sort of lens.

"And while I could order one online, I thought it would be better if I went and actually checked them out. Held them. See if I thought I could learn to use one. These aren't £99.00 specials. These are for professionals. So unless you'd like me here for the tourists, I thought I'd go look at cameras. Anne is attending with Derek and Damien so Beatrix knows she can ask her to help with refreshments or anything else for which she needs an extra pair of hands."

Thomas was starting to look abashed.

"And this fixation you're developing on whether I have a fixation on Marsh… I mean, get a grip, Thomas."

Thomas was routed. Maybe Chitta had a point about the best defence being a good offense, Maggie thought.

"Just make sure you bring me a proper invoice for the camera," Thomas said finally.

Maggie nodded while she grimaced internally. She had already bought one of the cameras David had recommended. And the receipt had the date on it. Well, she would wait and hope that by the time she gave it to Thomas he wouldn't check so closely. The price of the beast should distract him from the other details, she hoped.

She thought about what Crispin had said about her being a "Master of Deceit." Or perhaps that should be Mistress. Well, it was all for a righteous cause. And she could imagine Thomas' reaction if she'd said she wasn't going to the seminar because she and a former Special Forces commando and current government agent, all right, make that consulting government agent, were going to go explore Marsh's secret snowdrop garden. She'd find out if Beaumatin really did have a dungeon as Thomas sometimes teased. Because she was sure if he had any idea of her plans, he would promptly lock her up in it.

Chapter 15

Maggie had arranged to meet Crispin in the parking of a PC World in Oxford. They agreed her green Land Rover was too recognizable for her to leave it near Marsh's garden, which was not all that far away, and the car's presence would support her story about having been shopping for a camera.

"Very cloak and dagger," had been Maggie's comment.

Crispin had picked her up in a silver grey Ford Fiesta that embodied the notion of "inconspicuous."

They drove for half an hour through an increasingly rural landscape. There was no conversation. On a single-track lane, they entered some woods. On the left they were bordered by a stone wall. On the right they were open.

"We're here," said Crispin.

Maggie nodded. Her mouth was dry. She was definitely nervous.

"You're just going to go look at some snowdrops. Not steal the crown jewels. No biggie. Just remember to take deep breaths. Shallow breathing raises anxiety levels," she told herself.

Crispin pulled off the road onto a rutted track that led into the woods on the right. In a small clearing was an old caravan. Abandoned. Rusting. He pulled the car up beside it.

"All right. Show time."

They got out of the car. Crispin looked Maggie over. She was wearing a dark green turtleneck, a brown gilet, jeans and some well-worn Timberland boots.

"You'll do. You just need…"

He climbed into the caravan and returned with a brown watch cap.

"Put this on. With that hair you're recognisable for miles.

Maggie complied. She noted Crispin was wearing jeans, boots and a black leather biker jacket.

"No commando camouflage? Or face paint?"

Crispin laughed. "It's a woods in the Cotswolds, Moppet. We're not being parachuted behind enemy lines."

"And is there a plan?"

Crispin looked pained.

"I thought you knew…"

"Well, the main thing would be to see if he has any of the Beaumatin Blondes. Then there are the other varieties that went missing from Rochford Manor. Chloe Symeon. Esther Merton. Wasp…"

"Fine. I'll get us in. You check out your little flowers. I'll take pictures. You said you wanted pictures, right?"

"With the *Daily Post*?" Maggie tried to joke.

"Shucks. I forgot."

Maggie was looking worried.

"Don't be nervous, Moppet. It's a piece of cake. Your watchdogs haven't called?"

"No and we agreed no news is good news."

"Make sure your mobile is switched to vibrate."

Maggie made the adjustment and returned her mobile to her pocket.

"So I want to be out in twenty minutes or less. A couple of minutes in, fifteen to look around, then out. No dawdling. No wandering. Try not to leave footprints. Clear?"

"Clear."

"And no talking unless it's absolutely necessary. Although I must say, for a woman, I find you refreshingly unchatty."

Maggie gave Crispin her death glare.

They set off. As Maggie had feared, Crispin had to boost her over the wall, which was chest high. She came down hard on the other side and was brushing herself off while Crispin vaulted over effortlessly.

"I really need to join a gym," Maggie told herself.

He led her into the woods. As he had said, after about four hundred yards they emerged into a glade where the undergrowth had been cleared away. There were hundreds of snowdrops growing. Not naturalised, but in orderly plots of the same cultivars.

"That's where I saw the plants that had been recently put in," Crispin said in a low voice and pointed.

"All right. Take a picture, but we're looking for yellow. Six plants whose flowers have yellow streaks on the outer segments, er, petals." Maggie spoke quietly.

They searched the beds and were careful where they stepped. It was Maggie who found them.

"Crispin! Here!" She gestured.

They were indeed the Beaumatin's Blondes. All six plants. All blooming. Here was the proof.

"Take several pictures. Of the whole lot and some close ups. I'll keep looking."

Maggie found a plot of a dozen Chloe Symeons, whose six white segments formed a dainty globe.

"Take these too please," she asked Crispin.

Crispin was taking pictures when they heard a buzzing.

It continued.

Crispin checked a pocket and pulled out a small communications device.

"Fish?"

"What?"

"How close?"

"Okay. We're out of here. Stand by."

"What?"

"That was The Fish. He says Marsh just drove through the gate."

"What?"

"I thought you had eyes on him.

"I did. I do."

Maggie checked her mobile. Five missed calls. In her nervousness she had put the mobile on silent, not vibrate.

"Shit!"

There was the buzzing noise again.

"What!"

"Okay."

Crispin grabbed Maggie's arm and started running.

"We've got one minute to get out of here. Max."

They were barely out of sight of the snowdrop grove when Maggie heard yelling.

"Rotten kids! I'll get you!"

They reached the wall and Crispin lifted Maggie and practically tossed her over. She landed on her back on the other side.

Crispin sprang over and pulled her up.

"The caravan."

They sprinted the last hundred yards and hustled inside.

"This has been here for years. The Fish and I cleaned it up. Installed some... stuff." Nothing that would be noticed from outside."

Maggie looked around. She had never been in a caravan before. The inside was a bit shabby, but clean and tidy. There was a small, scarred wooden table and benches. A sofa, or perhaps it was a day bed, with a red plaid covering, ran across one side. A tiny kitchenette. A door she assumed hid a toilet. Some electronic equipment rested on a counter.

Maggie checked her mobile. The calls were all from Anne. Probably trying to warn her about Marsh. And the phone was definitely set to silent. Not vibrate.

Maggie held it out to Crispin.

"Anne tried to call. I accidentally set it to silent. Nerves. I'm sorry."

"In my work, accidentally can get you killed."

"I'm sorry. Really, really sorry."

Maggie heart was still racing and she was breathing rapidly. She put her hand to her chest. Crispin noticed.

"It's the effect of the adrenalin," he told her.

He removed her cap and her curls exploded.

"Adrenalin can also have other... stimulating effects," he said as he pulled her to him and kissed her.

He kissed her again and pushed her down on the sofa. And Maggie had to concede that adrenalin did have some stimulating effects. Very stimulating effects.

Crispin had Maggie thoroughly distracted when she suddenly became aware that he had peeled down her jeans and briefs and was about to...

"Oh no. Crispin. No. It's wrong. I can't. Please..."

"No, it's not. And yes, you can. And... too late."

Chapter 16

Maggie was distraught. Well, as distraught as she could be, given…

What had she done?

One thing was certain. Thomas must never, ever, under any circumstances, even on pain of death, find out.

Crispin had his arms wrapped around her and was watching her expressions change as they played across her face.

"Moppet, are you all right?"

Maggie tried to produce a smile that was not a grimace.

"Don't worry. What happens in the caravan, stays in the caravan. You don't have to be concerned about your file."

Maggie looked startled. She hadn't even thought of that.

"And I don't have anything, er, communicable."

Maggie looked even more startled.

"Um, I assume you don't either."

"No!"

Crispin studied her.

"You've never done this? Picked up someone in a pub? Answered a booty call? Hooked up at a club?"

"No. No. Remember, I'm Professor Margaret Spence Eliot. Renowned for being staid. Reserved. Aloof as well."

"Well, you seem to have achieved your secret identity, then. At least there was no aloof that I noticed."

Maggie looked back at Crispin. He really was terribly attractive. And amazing in other ways as well.

"Does this happen often? In your work?"

Crispin laughed.

"I wish."

"Oh."

"If it helps, think of this as a one off. Although technically I guess you'd have to call it a two off. Unless, of course, you'd like to make it a three off," and he leaned over and kissed her.

Later, Crispin dropped Maggie off at her car, still parked at PC World.

"I'll send you the pictures. And make some copies. And, although I guess in one sense it's 'Mission Accomplished,' I'm not sure a picture of your little yellow flowers is going to resolve your murders."

"I know. It's really only a first step. It proves there was a link between Marsh and Greenaway. What comes next..." she sighed.

"I don't suppose I could get a copy of the files on the murders? The police ones?"

"Hmm. I could ask Tim if I could show you what I have. Only the murder files, mind you. And I'll talk to Tim and see if he can extend my assignment. And if he might have any ideas about, um, next steps."

"You'd do that? Are you certain? This is hardly national security. In fact, I'm sure you must find it quite trivial compared to…"

"I would never call multiple murders trivial. If that's what they were. And having the perpetrator escape justice is certainly a security issue. Plus…" he paused.

"I'll let you know what Tim says. On the secure phone," he finished.

"Thank you, Crispin."

"Take care, Moppet."

"You too, Crispin."

He drove off.

Maggie thought, then went into the store and bought a second camera. She would just have to return the first one. After what had happened, she didn't want to take any chances with the receipt.

And just what had happened?

Well, the obvious.

And what should she do about that?

Well, she was certainly not going to tell Thomas. What the mind didn't know, the heart wouldn't grieve over, to adapt the phrase. Although, based on past experience, in Thomas' case his reaction wouldn't be grief, but a call to Simon Peevey to start divorce proceedings.

Well, forgiveness worked both ways, she supposed. She had certainly had to forgive Thomas. More than once. He would just have to forgive her. Even if he didn't know that he was forgiving her.

Anyway, it was the adrenaline.

"You are not a lesser woman, Maggie Eliot. Only a lesser woman would blame the adrenaline."

Force majeure?

Same thing. She had been a willing participant.

Yes, she had been,

She smiled.

"Get a grip, Eliot"

She got in the car and drove back to Beaumatin.

Mrs Cook reported that Lord Raynham had gone out with Cyril Westcott, the veterinarian. One of the lambs had scraped itself and the scrape had become infected. Supper could be served any time after Lord Raynham returned.

Maggie was sorry about the lamb but thankful for Thomas' absence. She left the camera in her study and went up to her room to shower and change.

Thomas came back. The lamb had had to be euthanized. The infection was too advanced.

"I'm sorry."

Thomas shrugged.

"I got a camera. I can show you after supper if you'd like."

Thomas nodded.

"I had to go to several places before I found the right model. And then this salesman—he looked like he was twenty if that—actually tried to talk me into buying a less expensive model. Can you believe that? I guess he thought the one I wanted would be too complicated for me.

"I know I'm doubtless older than his mother, but I'm certainly younger than his grandmother. Why would he assume I couldn't learn how to use it? It's only a camera after all, not a nuclear particle accelerator.

"Anyway, now I will have to learn how to use it. I hope David can give me a few tips. And then I'll need to learn about taking pictures of plants."

She noticed that Thomas had definitely tuned out.

"Thomas?"

"I'm sorry. I'm just tired."

"Oh dear. Then I'll stop nattering.

"No. That's all right. I like your... nattering."

Maggie looked more closely at Thomas. He did look tired.

"How were the snowdrop tourists?"

"It was nice to see Anne. Fiske and Hawking came. With a couple of clients, I think. Otherwise, same old, same old, as you'd say. Marsh had to run an emergency errand, I gather. Anyway, he didn't come. And I sensed Beatrix missed your support. I think it's getting harder for her. Without Charlotte. And Chloe not feeling well. It's just her and David. You should go on Friday if you can."

"Then I will. Definitely."

"You'll soon be able to play tour guide yourself."

"I probably could already. Provided no one asked any hard questions."

"It's not the hard questions. It's the stupid ones."

"There's no such thing as a stupid question."

"So you say."

Maggie put her hand on Thomas' arm.

"History channel? I can bring up some Laphroaig."

He put his hand over hers.

"Thank you."

He stood and kissed the top of her head.

"I'm glad you're here, Papillon."

Maggie thought that, at this point, a lesser woman would start writhing on the floor in paroxysms of guilt.

"But you are not a lesser woman. In addition, you are the Queen of Compartmentalisation. You can do this."

Chapter 17

Maggie called Anne and explained about her mistake.

"You need to be more careful. You had me scared to death!" Her friend was irate.

"I'm really sorry."

"Well, don't do it again."

"I promise. I won't."

They agreed to meet for lunch the next day at Digbeth's in Stowe on the Wold. It was by far their favourite teashop of the myriads that seemed to proliferate in the Cotswolds like bindweed in a garden.

"And I think Derek and Damien would like to come too."

"Of course."

Since it was February, it was not hard to find a table in the cosy restaurant. Shortly after Maggie and Anne arrived, Derek and Damien appeared.

"Tell us! We were frantic until you called," complained Damien.

"Yes. We imagined you were serving as lunch for a pack of Pit Bulls," added Derek.

"I'm really sorry. I was more nervous than I expected to be and I accidentally put my mobile on silent rather than vibrate. Fortunately my, um, technical support had a backup warning system in place. We got out just in time."

Maggie knew everyone had met Crispin—as Lennox—at the Snowdrop Ball, so she was not going say anything to reveal his identity.

"Just don't let it happen again," said Derek sternly.

"Again?" said Anne.

"And there were no Pit Bulls. Or Rottweilers. Or Dobermans. In fact, there is apparently no security at all. I wonder if Marsh didn't start those rumours himself," Maggie explained.

"So what was there?"

"Snowdrops. In the middle of a wood. Surrounded by a stone wall."

Maggie realised suddenly that she had no idea where Marsh's secret garden was. The route Crispin had taken had had many twists and turns. There was no way she could remember them all. Had that been on purpose, she wondered indignantly. So she couldn't go back on her own?

"Anyway, the Beaumatin Blondes were there. All six of them. And the Chloe Symeons that also went missing from Rochford Manor. And, the night of the Snowdrop Ball, when Marsh didn't show? There was a theft of snowdrops from a garden in Warwickshire. The owners were at the ball. And there was a patch of newly planted snowdrops in Marsh's garden. We think they're the ones that were stolen. I'll need to compare the picture with the list from the police to make sure, but…"

"Who's we? Do you really have some private eye you're working with? And how do you know what's in the police report?" Anne asked.

"Well, yes. I have help. Did you really think I could do all this on my own?"

"We think you could do anything you set your mind to, Maggie. Eliot. Er, Raynham," said Derek.

"Yes. Well, thank you. Anyway, now at least we know Marsh is a poacher. And a thief. Or a thief's accomplice."

Maggie remembered she had said nothing about the murders to her friends.

"So what are you going to do?" asked Damien.

"I'm not sure."

"Isn't finding your Beaumatin's Blonde in his lair enough to discredit him?"

"Perhaps. But I'm afraid he'll just say Greenaway gave them to him to 'distribute the risk.'"

"All six?"

"Yes. There is that. And since he's been to Beaumatin when Thomas has shown the Blonde to the Rochford seminar attendees, there's no way Marsh can claim he didn't know what they were.

"But. Well. Some of these collectors. I'm afraid they'd deal with him no matter how unscrupulous he was shown to be."

"How about the ones you say that were just stolen?"

"Yes. I've been thinking about that. And I'm told that there are tests for soil that can prove where a plant came from. And the bulbs would definitely have traces of soil from the

Warwickshire garden. Quite a bit of soil, as I assume he would have tried not to disturb the root balls."

Maggie sighed.

"Anyhow, thanks for all your help. I'll let you know what's happening."

"And if there's anything else we can do," said Damien.

Oh. Wait. There is. I wondered... Well. Since Thomas has been showing Beaumatin's Blonde to the people from the Rochford Manor seminars, I thought... Well, maybe it should be announced publically. So there's no way Marsh can try to pre-empt... claim it was his own discovery. Like a scientist tries to get his work published in a journal before anyone else can take credit.

"But of course I can't do it myself. So I wondered... Do either of you know Mark Deacon?"

"The famous botanical blogger? Well, we don't go on hols together. But we know who he is. And he knows who we are. Why?" said Derek.

"If I sent you a photo of Beaumatin's Blonde. And a text. Could you pass it on to him? It's the sort of thing he'd mention. But it needs to look like it comes from you."

"I don't see why not," said Damien.

"Great. I'll send you something as soon as I get home."

"Anyone for pudding? They're famous here. And the custard sauce is to die for," said Anne.

Chapter 18

Maggie returned to Beaumatin to find Thomas was out with the sheep.

Of course, it seemed like Thomas was always out with the sheep. And Ned.

Sheep had little interest for Maggie. She had decided in her role as Lady Raynham she would focus on the gardens and Thomas would have to be happy with that. And of course apparently being a best-selling author. How did she feel about that?

How she felt about that did not come close to making the list of things she was wondering how she felt about. Or was trying hard not to feel about.

Maggie went to the greenhouse and used her smart phone to take a picture of the Beaumatin's Blonde that Thomas had shown to the visitors from Rochford Manor. It might not be Marsh quality, but it was good enough. Using the new Nikon would have to wait. It was going to take her a week just to read the instruction manual.

She sent the picture to Derek and Damien with a text.

"Visitors from this year's Rochford Manor Snowdrop Seminar had a surprise when they visited the gardens at Beaumatin as part of their study day. They were treated to a view of a remarkable new snowdrop. Called Beaumatin's Blonde, it is unique in having significant deep yellow streaking on its outer segments as well as having inner segments that are also nearly solid yellow. Although Beaumatin's Blonde is being propagated, it will still be a few years before plants are ready for wider distribution. We are sure galanthophiles will be eagerly awaiting news of its availability."

"Please let me know when you've sent this off and if you get any response from Deacon. And I'll watch the blog," she added.

Maggie found she had received two emails from unknown addresses. Both had attachments. Normally she would have automatically deleted them except for their subject matter.

The first was titled "Dragon's Lair" and the files were jpegs. She clicked on one and hoped if there were a problem with the file her anti-virus software would sound an alarm.

It was a picture of a clump of Chloe Symeon. From Marsh's garden. They were the photos from Crispin. Good. She created a file and copied the pictures into it.

She sent back a return email. "Thanks."

Almost immediately she got a reply. "Undeliverable. Addressee unknown."

Well, she should have figured.

The second email was titled, "Burn after reading." That sounded like it could be from Crispin as well. The attachments were a series of pdf files. Again, she hoped her Norton was good enough to detect any problem.

There was no threat detected and the pdfs were scans of the police files of the three deaths. Verney. Walker. Greenaway. She realised the reports were written by Jack Patrick, her "tame" inspector's sergeant, and signed by Willis. The pathologist's autopsy reports were included.

They would make grim bedtime reading. Not that with Thomas she got much chance for that. And she certainly couldn't read them while he was watching *Band of Brothers*. Or David Attenborough. If she tried that, she wouldn't need to burn them, as she was sure Thomas himself would toss them into the nearest fire. And since it was February, he would have several choices.

Should she print them out? First she would save all the files on her hard drive, then to a USB stick as well. Then she would make print outs and then she would delete the emails. If more precautions were needed, tough tuna. She really didn't like this cloak and dagger stuff. And it seemed she wasn't very good at it, anyway.

She looked at the snowdrop pictures. They were good. There was no doubt those were the Beaumatin's Blondes. Had Crispin taken a course in plant photography, she wondered. Or was knowing how to take a decent picture under pressure another requirement in his line of work?

She printed out the police files. Pages and pages. She had to refill the paper tray of her printer and noticed a warning message that one of her cartridges was running out of ink. Fortunately, she kept a spare.

Maggie saw that the files contained pictures of the victims. Oh dear. Well, she supposed she didn't have to look at them. And she had seen Charlotte. And Walker. And had been there when Greenaway had…

Grim. Too much death. And for some small white flowers? Well, if her understanding of military history were correct, many more men had died for just as stupid reasons. World War I came to mind. She would have to ask Thomas what he thought. Then realised she couldn't. At least until this was over. She sighed.

Her mobile made the sounds it did when she got an SMS. She didn't recognise the number.

"Mission extended. C."

Oh. That was good news. Well, complicated. But good.

What should she reply? A happy face? Ugh. All right.

"Good news."

A reply came quickly.

"Meet tomorrow?"

"Yes. Where?"

"Caravan?"

She was sure Crispin was grinning.

"No. Besides I don't know where it is."

"You're not supposed to."

Grrr. Maggie thought. She was apparently too well known in the Cotswolds. She had just been to Oxford.

"I will have to think about where."

"Tomorrow, then. I'll have a think as well."

There were no more messages. Maggie carefully deleted the exchange. Yes. She really hated this cloak and dagger stuff.

Maggie checked the time. If Thomas stuck to routine, she had an hour before he returned. Then he would want to shower and change out of his riding clothes. Thomas was fairly predictable that way. Maggie wondered if she were as predictable. Maybe. But then again, maybe not.

Maggie decided to start with Charlotte's file. The one about which she cared the most. But first, she took a couple of journal articles she had printed out from one of her shelves to have at hand to conceal what she was reading if there were any unexpected interruptions. Then she buried the other two police reports in another stack of printouts. The world may have gone digital, but when she had to make notes or comment on an article, she wanted paper.

The file made sad reading. She was mentioned, of course, as Lady Raynham. She was interested to note that there was no doubt the cause of death was hanging. The marks made by the rope were not a cover-up of some other act. Charlotte had been alive when she had hanged herself—or was hanged—from that tree branch. Alive but drugged. The autopsy revealed significant quantities of barbiturates in her bloodstream. The theory was that she had taken them to make her death easier. To minimize any struggling.

However, the police had never discovered any of the drug in Charlotte's small apartment in the Manor. Which she had shared with Emily. Her doctor insisted he had never prescribed any and none of the local pharmacies had any records of such a prescription.

Maggie wondered if the police had checked Walker or Greenaway or Marsh to see if they might have ever been prescribed barbiturates. The report gave no indication and it had been weeks between the deaths of Charlotte and Walker. By which time Charlotte's wretched end had been ruled a suicide. So there would have been no reason to look.

And by now, Greenaway's cottage on the Rochford Manor estate had been cleared out. Maggie had no idea what had happened to Linda's flat that was above her shop. Had her sister come to undertake the sad task of dealing with her things? Of course, Marsh's place was still a possibility. Would a break-in be within Crispin's skillset? She could imagine his reaction.

In addition, Maggie wondered if the dose of barbiturates had been enough to render Charlotte unconscious. She had no idea of knowing from the figures. She'd have to ask Crispin that as well. She should make a list.

She also wanted to go back to Marsh's garden. The problem being, if she went with Crispin, there was the issue of its proximity to the caravan. She knew there was no way she could ever go there with him again.

However…

She remembered Crispin saying the land was still registered in Marsh's grandmother's name. What was it? Could she remember? It was something she had associated with gardens when he'd said it. With… Jekyll. Gertrude Jekyll. The famous garden designer. So Marsh's grandmother's name was Gertrude… What? Gertrude who? Gertrude… Could it be Jenkins? She thought he'd said Jenkins. Like Gertrude Jekyll. Gertrude Jenkins. At least she thought it had been Gertrude Jenkins. Gertrude Jenkins who had died thirty years ago. And had a daughter, Serena.

She would send an email to Maddy Rana, a solicitor who worked with Simon Peevey and specialised in contracts. Swear her to secrecy. And ask if she could do a property search. Or maybe get Simon to do one. Without knowing who was asking.

"Oh what a tangled web we weave, when first we practice to deceive," thought Maggie. Sir Walter Scott wrote that, she remembered, although it was often wrongly attributed to the Bard of Avon.

She sent the email to Maddy anyway. She assumed the land was in Oxfordshire or Gloucestershire. She wondered how long a title search would take. If the counties' records had been digitised it would be easier. She could imagine the time it would take someone to go to Gloucester or Oxford and search through decades of undoubtedly dusty and crumbling files.

While Maggie was contemplating more "next steps," another email arrived. It was from Malcolm Fortescue-Smythe.

"Congratulations, Best Seller," it was titled.

Apparently The Global Press had never had one of its publications on the bestseller list before. Malcolm wanted to organise a celebratory lunch in London and discuss how the success of Maggie's volume might be replicated. He knew it was short notice, but might she be free the next day? Had she liked the Arts Club?

Hmm. She sent an SMS to Crispin.

"I have been asked to lunch in Mayfair tomorrow. Meet you at the Dorchester bar at 15:00ish?"

"Works for me. I'll be the one holding a red rose."

Maggie was fairly sure Thomas had nothing he needed her for on Wednesday. She accepted Malcolm's invitation.

Chapter 19

Maggie was full of Dover sole and some very fine white Burgundy. She had resisted the temptation to inquire after Tatiana and instead had focussed on whether she thought any of the volumes contemplated for the Developing World series had the potential of her current opus.

"Possibly the one on China. The one that Stephen Draycott and one of his Chinese colleagues will be writing. Probably not Eunice's on Post-Colonialism, although I expect that to generate significant interest among the usual suspects. Since it's snowdrop season, I've been a bit distracted. I'll be able to give this more serious thought in a week or two," she assured Malcolm.

"How about a book on snowdrops? They seem to be the current rage," he asked, only half facetiously.

Maggie laughed. "Well, the best ever book written on snowdrops has never made the best seller list. Of course it costs £65, so that might be a factor. Let me think about it."

Crispin was already at a table with some whisky when Maggie entered the bar. He was wearing a wonderful suit by some major Italian designer and was attracting some attention from a group at a nearby table whom Maggie classified as "Yummy Mummies." She hoped they wouldn't assume she was his mother. Or aunt.

But she was wearing a very chic dark blue Ralph Lauren suit herself and, after her best-selling author lunch, was feeling very kickass. And Malcolm had asked if she'd like him to propose her for Arts Club membership.

She had been surprised and flattered, but laughed and said, "Thank you very much, Malcolm, but no." So bring it on, Yummy Mummies.

Crispin rose and regarded her appreciatively.

"Which identity are you today? Not the professor. And not Lady Raynham."

"No. It's the author. I've just come from the Arts Club. Lunch with my appreciative publisher."

"Fortescue-Smythe?"

Maggie nodded.

"How's the delicious Tatiana?"

"Somehow I neglected to ask."

Crispin laughed. He signalled to a waiter and ordered some Viognier for Maggie.

She raised her eyebrows.

"What? You would have preferred a Cosmopolitan?"

She shook her head.

When the wine had been served, Crispin said, "So what's new?"

"I read the files you sent."

"Grim reading."

"Very. Worse if you knew the people."

Crispin nodded.

"Anyway, I did have some questions. In fact, I made a list."

Maggie dug in her briefcase and handed Crispin a sheet of paper.

"So here they are. Most pertain to Charlotte. A couple to Linda Walker. And of course, Marsh was not a factor in the investigation into Charlotte's death but I have a few about him as well. Like had he ever been prescribed barbiturates? And if you searched his house, would it be possible there'd be a bottle in a medicine cabinet somewhere?"

Now it was Crispin's turn to raise his brows.

"I see I've created a monster."

"Sorry. And you take too much credit. I'm afraid asking questions is a long-standing habit."

"Your students must have a love-hate relationship with their tutor."

Maggie laughed. "You may be right there. And that works both ways."

"Let's look at this list."

He read down. Nodded. Frowned. Nodded. Shook his head.

"I can take a look at Marsh's financials. And I can try to do a search on barbiturate prescriptions. And on your questions about the dosage—whether Charlotte could have been unconscious. Tracing the rope? That would be extremely difficult, time consuming and, in the end, probably inconclusive. Now this…" he tapped the paper.

"You want to break into Marsh's house? The garden wasn't enough for you?"

"I know. Grasping at straws."

"Well it's been six months since Verney... died. And as you know, the police never looked at Marsh as being connected with any of these deaths. Finding anything at this point..."

"So I assume you've read the files. With the idea that Marsh could have been a factor. What would you do?"

Crispin became reflective.

"In my... line of work, we identify a desired end result and then work backwards to see how that could be achieved."

"Oh. Well, I guess my desired end would be to have Charlotte's death declared not a suicide and for Marsh... not to be able to cause any more damage. Since at this point he seems to be beyond the reach of the legal system."

"I assume you wouldn't consider just removing this particular piece from the board?"

Maggie was shocked and it showed. She looked at Crispin who was observing her closely. She wondered again exactly what it was that he did for Tim.

"No. You're right. I wouldn't," she said flatly.

Crispin took her hand, lifted it, and kissed it.

"Good answer, Moppet. I didn't think I was wrong about you."

He flagged a waiter and ordered more Laphroaig and Viognier.

Maggie continued, "That being said. What's a best-case scenario at this point? We can prove Marsh has the Beaumatin Blondes. And the Chloe Symeons. But he could always say he received them from Greenaway in good faith.

"We could prove he stole the Epsleys snowdrops. For which he'd probably have to, what, pay a fine? Lose face among the galanthophile set? I'm sure there are still collectors who would deal with him if it meant obtaining a cultivar they coveted and he could provide."

"You're looking for justice? Tilting at windmills, my sweet."

Maggie put out her hand and he took it. They sat in silence for some moments.

"So?" she asked.

"I need to think. I'll try to get that information on those barbiturates. And the effects of the dosage. And maybe I'll do some digging on Marsh. I'll be in touch. And you know how to reach me."

"Yes I do. *1."

Crispin laughed without much humour.

SUSAN ALEXANDER

Chapter 20

Maggie pressed *1.

"Crispin? Where are you?"

"Um. England?"

"I'm serious. I need to see you."

Crispin caught Maggie's tone.

"Maggie, are you all right?"

"Well, there has been a… development."

"If I came to you, where would I go?"

Maggie thought. She was at Anne's in Broadway. She needed a place she could hope she wouldn't be recognised.

"There's a village. Upper Edmond. In Gloucestershire. The Cotswolds. It's where my borrowed writer's block cottage was located. It has a pub. I never went in. Could we meet there? Could you find it?"

"Are you sure you couldn't find someplace further off the beaten track?"

"If I knew of such a place, I would have suggested it."

There was a pause.

"It will take me two hours. Maybe three."

"I'm sorry. I assure you, this is not trivial."

"It's all right. I didn't think it was."

Maggie had another cup of Anne's excellent coffee. She admired her friend's newest additions to her wardrobe. She caught up on the latest doings of Anne's three sons. Time passed slowly. Finally she left for the pub.

Maggie had borrowed a kind of head covering from Anne. Anne called it her "schmatta." Maggie thought that given the multiple three figures the piece of dark blue cloth had probably cost, there must be a better term. But Maggie figured her hair was her most conspicuous feature and, since she really wanted to avoid being recognised, she should at least cover it. And as the weather continued to be wintry, a hat or whatever this was would not seem inappropriate.

It took Crispin three hours. Waiting at the pub, Maggie had mentioned to the barmaid she was expecting a friend, but after an hour had passed and no one appeared, she had begun to get curious looks.

Crispin needed a moment to recognise her.

"Incognito?"

She smiled. "You can try for Laphroaig, but you might want to have a backup choice."

Crispin settled for a lesser whisky and returned to the table.

"So what's this… development?"

Maggie looked at Crispin. Took a deep breath.

"I went back to Marsh's garden."

Crispin became still. His face revealed nothing but his hard eyes narrowed.

"I thought I had your promise…"

"For our previous visit. Which as you know was cut short."

"How did you even find it?"

"You'd mentioned that the land was in the name of Marsh's grandmother. Gertrude Jenkins. It helped that she shares a name with a famous garden designer. Gertrude Jekyll. I remembered it. And some other details."

Crispin grimaced.

"I had a title search done. The records are in a database. It took less than an hour to find."

Crispin's grimace became a scowl.

"Well. I guess I underestimated you," he said finally.

"And if you think I was being reckless… Marsh has a website. Among other content, it has a calendar of where he's speaking. This morning he gave a talk in Cambridgeshire. Too far for him to make a quick dash back to pick up an order he'd forgotten. I checked to make sure he'd turned up. And Anne Brooks came with me to keep watch.

"I went because we had no pictures of the snowdrops from the Epsley garden. And once the flowers are gone and the plants have settled in, it will be hard to prove that they were the ones taken. Or even which cultivar they were. Until next year.

"But that's not what's important."

"Oh no?" Crispin's tone was cool. Maggie sensed how angry he was but she went ahead anyway.

"In for a penny, in for a pound," she told herself.

"Because of the weather—snow, freezing temperatures—it's becoming harder for wildlife to find food. I've read advisories suggesting people put out bird food..."

Crispin made an impatient gesture.

"Sorry. Anyway, animals, deer, for instance, which tend to be a scourge of gardeners, don't eat snowdrop bulbs. But when Marsh planted the Epsley snowdrops, well, it seems some animal took advantage of the loosened dirt and went digging looking for... well, for something to eat I suppose. And I found something... somethings that had been turned up. From the soil. They're in my car. Let me show you."

Both glasses were empty. Crispin got up and followed Maggie outside.

Maggie had a Waitrose bag in her car boot. She gestured and Crispin looked inside.

"You said you thought the place had an ugly feel. And those are what I think they are, right?"

In the bag were bones. A vertebra, a rib, a tibula and some small bones that looked like bits of fingers.

"I know I should have left them in place, but I was afraid if Marsh came back, that he'd remove them. I did take some pictures."

Maggie waited for Crispin's reaction, but he said nothing. He simply picked up the bag, closed the trunk and took Maggie's arm.

"Let's go."

"But..."

"Expected home? I'm sure you'll come up with a good story to tell his lordship."

He led her to a gleaming black Porsche and opened the passenger door.

"What happened to the Fiesta?"

"Eliot. Just… Shut up."

Maggie knew when to keep quiet.

Crispin made a call.

"Fish? Are you still tracking the Gnat? I need a location. All right. Call me back."

With Crispin taking a direct route this time, it took them less than twenty minutes to arrive at the caravan.

Crispin climbed in. Maggie hesitated.

"There are things I need. Believe me, I'm not feeling amorous."

Maggie followed him into the caravan.

Crispin was putting various pieces of equipment into a backpack.

"Should I put on a cap? Or is this all right?" she asked.

"No. You're not going to need one," he said from behind her.

Without warning, he wrapped one arm tightly around her and with his other hand pressed against the side of her neck. Maggie struggled but Crispin was strong and, in moments, she was unconscious.

Sometime later, Maggie came to. Confused. What had happened? Where was she?

Things came into focus.

The caravan. Crispin. He'd....

Maggie tried to figure out how long she'd been unconscious. The light inside the caravan was dim. Was it because it was overcast or was the sun setting?

She was on the sofa. She tried to move and realised her hands and feet were tied together behind her back. Hog-tied. And she was gagged.

Maggie felt angry. Really angry that Crispin would do something like this. She had trusted him.

Minutes passed and Maggie began to panic. What if something happened to Crispin? What if he never came back? How could she get help? Who would find her? She had to try to get out of the caravan.

She rocked from side to side until she fell with a crash onto the floor.

Ow. That hurt. She'd have bruises.

Yes. But no one would see them when all that was left of her were bones.

Maggie was becoming hysterical. She began wriggling towards the door like a caterpillar. She was moving an inch at a time. She felt like her arms were going to be torn out of their sockets.

She was half way to the door when it opened and Crispin climbed in.

"Maggie!"

He bent and scooped her up and deposited her back on the sofa.

Tears were streaming down her cheeks and her nose was running.

Crispin pulled out a handkerchief and wiped her face. Then he reached under his jacket and pulled out a vicious-looking hunting knife.

"Don't move," he said.

Maggie recoiled in terror.

"Maggie. It's all right. I'm just going to cut you loose."

He cut through the cords.

Hands free and feet free, Maggie attacked, punching his chest.

He grabbed her hands and held her. She fought him.

"Stop it, Moppet. It's all right."

He pulled down the gag.

"How could you... how could you... I was afraid... I was afraid something would happen... That you wouldn't come back and that I'd..."

Maggie sobbed. He held her.

"I had to know you were going to stay put. There was no time to argue. And I couldn't trust you not to try to follow me."

Crispin didn't add that if he hadn't been so furious with her he might have been less brutal.

"And The Fish knows where we are."

Maggie was still distraught, so Crispin did the only other thing he could think of. He was only human, after all.

Chapter 21

Maggie had fallen asleep on the drive back to the pub where her car was parked.

"Moppet? We're here."

"Oh. I'm sorry."

Silence.

"So what now?"

Crispin hadn't told Maggie that not only had he seen more bones where the Epsley snowdrops had been planted, but that he'd also noticed two other rectangular spots where the ground was sunken, a tell-take indicator that there might be other bodies buried in the glade.

He hadn't spotted them on his previous visits, as he had been focussing on the snowdrops, but obviously his subconscious had noticed. Which is why he had had the bad feeling he did about the place.

"Our problem is I can't just call up your Inspector Willis and say, 'I just happened to be strolling in some woods, which incidentally were obviously private property because they were walled in, and found some bones.' And it would be even more of a problem if you told him. I gather he knows your feelings about Marsh."

Maggie nodded.

"Anyhow, let me talk to Tim."

Maggie nodded.

"Moppet, are you all right?"

"Yes. I'm all right. I'm fine."

Crispin looked sceptical.

"But may I borrow your mobile?"

Maggie got out of the car and dialled a number.

Crispin heard, "Mrs Cook? It's, er, Lady Raynham. I'm just leaving Anne Brooks' house. My phone died. It needs to be recharged. Is Lord Raynham... He's out? All right. When he comes in, please let him know I'll be home soon."

She leaned in and handed the phone back to Crispin.

"I really hated doing that."

"I imagine you would."

Crispin drove off and Maggie got in the Land Rover. She dialled Anne.

"Anne? If anyone ever asks. Although I don't expect they will. But anyway, short of perjury, this afternoon we went for a long walk. We got lost. We were out of range of a phone tower. And I'm just leaving your house."

"Got it, girlfriend. Are you all right?"

"Yes. And I'll tell you everything tomorrow. No, wait, it's a seminar day again and I'm helping out. Saturday, then."

Maggie turned off her phone and drove off.

Left Brain: Well. Again?

Right Brain: Not a word! Not one word!

Chapter 22

Maggie had gotten back to Beaumatin in time to shower, change her clothes and assess the damage from falling over the wall—twice—in Marsh's garden and her struggle in the caravan. It was not pretty.

When she came down for dinner, Thomas took one look and said, "Good God. What happened to you?"

"Anne is on a fitness kick and decided to take a long walk in the country. We got lost. I fell. More than once. It's harder climbing over a fence than you'd think. And going uphill. And downhill. When there's undergrowth."

Thomas' mouth twitched. He ruffled her curls. "Mon pauvre papillon."

Maggie felt like she was going to expire from guilt.

She arrived at Rochford Manor for the final seminar early. She ached and was a mass of assorted scrapes and bruises. She had a cut on her forehead that no amount of foundation was going to cover, so she simply put a plaster over it. If anyone minded, tough tuna.

Maggie wished there was a setting for triple espresso on the coffee machine. She was going to need a lot of caffeine to make it through the day. And aspirin. Beatrix announced the seminar was fully booked and there were some sizeable advance orders for Rochford Manor snowdrops. She looked pleased.

Then she looked at Maggie more closely.

"What happened to you, my dear? You look like you were in a pub brawl and lost."

Maggie explained about Anne and the walk.

"Humpf," was Beatrix's comment.

People began to arrive. It was the usual assortment of prosperous women with some men in their fifties and sixties and even seventies. Then Maggie heard Beatrix exclaim, "Lennox? What brings you here? I was expecting to see your aunt."

Maggie whirled around and saw Crispin coming through the door.

She stared. He was wearing the brown corduroy pants he had worn in Oxford, but with a plaid shirt and a brown tweed shooting jacket. Today's disguise was galanthophile, she decided.

"Lady Ainswick. Lady Sarah sends her apologies. But… sciatica. It was acting up and she asked me to come in her stead. She gave me an order for some snowdrops. I hope it's still possible to fill it. It would cheer her up."

He pulled a piece of paper from a pocket and handed it to Beatrix.

Beatrix scanned the list.

"I'll give this to David. David Osborne, my son-in-law. I'm sure we can provide you with these. And please tell Lady Sarah how sorry I am she's not feeling well."

"And I'm to sit in on the lectures and take notes."

"You're more than welcome. There are also tours of the gardens here and of Beaumatin, Lord Raynham's estate. In fact, here's Lady Raynham. I believe you met her at our recent dance."

Maggie nodded to Crispin, no he was Lennox today. She could tell he was trying not to laugh and she repressed an urge to kick him.

Beatrix went off to greet some other new arrivals.

"Are you interested in snowdrops, Mr Archibald-Atherton?" Maggie asked in tones that could etch glass.

"My aunt professes to be. And even though I suspect it's just because it's so fashionable currently, I feel obliged to humour her."

"Favourite nephew?"

"Only nephew."

He noticed the plaster on Maggie's forehead and some bruises and scrapes on her hands.

"Did you have an accident, Lady Raynham? Horse bolt?"

Maggie decided it would be more dignified not to answer. She noticed a pitcher that needed refilling and carried it off to the kitchen.

David gave his lecture, followed by his species pub quiz. Halfway through, Marsh came in. He was wearing his typical outfit, complete with Highgrove bag, and his hair needed a wash as usual. Maggie wondered how it was possible to always be one day beyond needing a shampoo. Of course she didn't see him every day. Or perhaps this was his public persona. Did Marsh have a secret identity like he had a secret garden?

And what was Crispin, er, Lennox doing here? Was this part of some plan he'd concocted? Then she wondered if he had ever actually met Marsh. Face-to-face. Perhaps that was why he had come.

The quiz ended and Maggie was surprised to note that Crispin's team had won. And apparently was giving the credit to Crispin. He accepted a Magnet from David.

"I'm sure Aunt Sarah will appreciate it and be pleased that those hours we have spent together in her garden have not been wasted."

"Laying it on a bit thick, aren't you, Crispin?" Maggie thought to herself.

David began the tour of the Rochford Manor gardens. Maggie tagged along at the back. She saw how Crispin, who had begun the walk near the front of the group with David, had gradually dropped back until he was in the rear with Marsh.

Marsh's coterie was smaller today than it had been the first week. Just a single couple were hanging on his words. When they paused to admire a display of Lord Lieutenants, Crispin glanced back at Maggie and gave a quick jerk of his head towards the pair.

Maggie deduced that Crispin wanted some private time with Marsh, so she moved in on the couple. She introduced herself as Lady Raynham, which immediately produced a positive response.

Maggie guessed that, in addition to being older, prosperous and Anglo, there were very few Republicans who attended snowdrop seminars.

Mr and Mrs Foxcroft were from Taunton and were avid galanthophiles.

Mrs Foxcroft said they had read Mark Deacon's most recent blog that had had a post about the Beaumatin's Blonde. With a picture.

"What an exquisite snowdrop. And so unusual. Will we see some this afternoon on our visit?"

"They are still being propagated. But I'm sure Lord Raynham plans to show it," Maggie explained.

"Are any for sale?" asked Mr Foxcroft eagerly.

"Not yet, I'm afraid," said Maggie.

"Would you put us on a waiting list? Like Nat does?" asked Mrs Foxcroft.

"If you'd provide me with your contact information, I'll inform you as soon as any are available."

"Thank you. We realise a Galanthus like that won't come cheap. But it would be worth every pound."

Maggie wondered if Marsh also had a waiting list for a Beaumatin's Blonde. She noticed Crispin having a low-voiced but intense conversation with the snowdropiteer, as Derek had called him.

At first Marsh frowned and shook his head. Crispin continued, then reached in a pocket and handed Marsh a folded piece of paper. Marsh opened it. Stopped dead. Smiled an oily smile.

To distract the Foxcrofts from Crispin and Marsh, Maggie continued, "There is another rare snowdrop at Beaumatin. Beaumatin's Harriet. A beautiful double yellow. Do you know it? It is supposed to be offered through Rochford Manor beginning next year."

Mrs Foxcroft looked interested. "A double yellow? Yes, we would indeed be buyers."

Crispin continued his monologue. Finally Marsh shrugged, then nodded. The men shook hands and Crispin moved off.

Chapter 23

At lunch, Crispin sat with Lady Ainswick. He entertained the table, which erupted in frequent laughter. Afterwards, Beatrix confided to Maggie, "That Lennox Archibald-Atherton is certainly a charmer. We need more young men like him at the seminars. Do any of his generation garden, do you know?"

"We could put an ad on Craig's list," Maggie suggested.

Beatrix looked confused.

The day, which had begun chilly and overcast, had brightened in time for the tour of Beaumatin. The group happily followed Thomas through the gardens and the Foxcrofts exclaimed with the others at both Beaumatin's Harriet and Beaumatin's Blonde.

Maggie hung back and observed Crispin, who was again walking with Marsh. As they passed through the rose garden on their way to the areas beyond, Crispin pulled Marsh aside and seemed to ask a question. But Maggie saw him nod quite clearly at the door in the wall. Marsh stared, and then looked around as though to orient himself.

What was he doing? Maggie was shocked that Crispin was aware of the door and thus obviously of Beaumatin's own "secret garden" which lay behind it and, even more, that he would share that knowledge with Marsh.

Was this some scheme of Crispin's to try to trap Marsh into incriminating himself? But in this case, didn't the risks outweigh the rewards? Alerting Marsh to the garden's location was certainly letting the fox into the henhouse. And wasn't there something called entrapment? Did they have entrapment in the UK? Of course, Crispin was not a policeman. Did that make a difference?

She had certainly not said anything about the place to Crispin, so how did he know? And if Thomas found out…

But what most concerned her was the Ainswick Orange. No one should know the plant was at Beaumatin except the Ainswicks, Thomas and herself. Of course, Crispin would have no way of knowing that the mythic plant was behind that door. And immediately identifiable, since it was blooming.

Maggie decided she would have to talk to Crispin. The next day was Saturday. But where?

The tour finished and the group returned to Rochford Manor for Marsh's lecture which, as previously, was practiced and informative. When he had finished and tea and coffee were being served, Maggie approached Crispin and said quietly, "We need to talk."

"I always dread it when I hear a woman say that," was Crispin's immediate reply.

"What do you think you're doing?"

"Setting a trap. Now I think you should go and refill this pitcher with milk."

Crispin handed her the jug.

Maggie felt on the verge of a tantrum. What was she? Three? This man was definitely a bad influence on her in all sorts of ways, in addition to….

Then she reminded herself she was not a lesser woman, so she smiled and went off for some milk.

Pitcher refilled, Maggie went outside to help David with plant sales. As before, all the more expensive varieties sold out first. Beatrix had explained that the Magnets and Comets and S Arnotts and even the basic nivalis were more popular on the weekends, when busloads of visitors would come to the Manor to see the snowdrops in bloom. The seminar attendees were the galanthophiles with the time and means to buy their Diggorys and Green Brushes to add to their collections.

Maggie watched Marsh go to his aging Volkswagen Golf TDI and open the boot. He took out a box with at least a dozen snowdrops and carried it over to the Foxcrofts. The couple excitedly examined the plants and then handed over a large wad of cash, which Marsh carefully counted before he nodded and closed the boot.

Maggie wondered about the man again. He seemed so... innocuous. It was hard to believe he could also be, well, completely evil. It seemed there was a super villain lurking beneath his shabby exterior.

Crispin was one of the first to leave. She noted he was driving his Porsche. When the last lingering visitor had departed, Ian appeared and helped David take the plants back to the greenhouse.

Maggie went to find Beatrix. Her friend looked frazzled.

"Well. Are you pleased?"

"I'm pleased that after the visitors' day tomorrow, that's it for another year. I seem to have less and less energy. And patience. Especially for stupid questions. You'd think if someone were paying £85 to attend a snowdrop seminar she'd already know the difference between a Galanthus and a Leucojum."

Maggie laughed. "Thomas said the same thing. About stupid questions. And I told him there are no stupid questions."

"Yes. But perhaps that's why you're a professor."

"In fact, many of my colleagues have no tolerance for them either."

"I'm just so thankful David is here. And Chloe, when she's feeling better. And you must thank Thomas for sparing us Ian. He's been so helpful."

"I think he's really interested in the snowdrops. I sense he'd like to do more than just weed and fertilise and do the more menial chores."

"Then we should talk about that. David has said he'd like to have the opportunity to be a mentor."

Maggie nodded and hoped Thomas would be equally supportive of having one of his groundsmen move on to better things.

"I believe both he and Wesley will be here tomorrow to help with the hoards."

Maggie gave Beatrix a hug, and then drove off.

As soon as Maggie was on the grey road that led to Beaumatin, she pulled over and called Crispin on the secure phone.

"Hey, Moppet."

"Crispin, what exactly are you doing with Marsh? I'd really like to know."

"Let's exercise a little discretion, please."

"Sorry. But same question."

"Um. Maybe we should meet."

"Yes. Definitely. But when? And where?"

"Tomorrow? The caravan? Now that you know where it is."

"No!"

Maggie thought.

"The Oxford PC World. In the parking. Two o'clock. And perhaps you could drive something a bit less conspicuous than your Porsche."

"Moppet, you're no fun at all."

"Fun would need a whole other secret identity at this point."

"All right."

"I'll be the one holding the red rose."

"See. I knew you could be fun."

"Argh."

Maggie ended the call.

As she drove back to Beaumatin, Maggie tried to think of a reason she needed to return to the store.

Aha. She was sure she could use a second battery and memory card for the new camera. But first she had better figure out how to use the ones she had. It wouldn't do to have two batteries she didn't know how to charge. Or where they fit in the Nikon.

Back at Beaumatin, Maggie went right to her study and found the camera's instruction manual. It was thick enough to make a good doorstop. She was relieved to find a section on "Getting Started."

She began charging the battery and continued reading. The camera was not radically different than her old Nikon, which she thought was in a box somewhere in the Hereford Crescent house. Except it was different. It could record video. And you could instantly see what your pictures looked like. Keep what you wanted and delete what you didn't. No waiting for film to be developed.

"Oh brave new world," Maggie muttered.

She was not going to be defeated, she vowed. Numquam cede. Never give up. She repeated the Raynham motto like a mantra.

At supper she told Thomas, "I've been learning to use the camera. But it seems I need a second battery and an extra memory card. The callow youth at PC World neglected to impart this information. So if it's all right, I'll dash over tomorrow afternoon and pick them up. I checked and they're in stock."

Thomas nodded. "I'll probably be out with Ned."

He looked at his wife.

"You really think you're going to be able to learn how to do this? I checked. It's not a simple instrument."

"I have a fairly decent Nikon that's non-digital. And in my youth I took a couple of photography courses. One when I was in high school. To enhance my attractiveness for college admissions. To show I was well-rounded.

174

"I would have thought you'd have gotten into any college you chose."

"You can never be too sure, was my parents' attitude."

"Humpf."

"And then I took a course one summer while I was in college. I was interested in anthropology at that point. I wanted to be the next Margaret Mead. And thought it would be good to know how to take pictures when I discovered some lost tribe in the Amazon.

"But then I found out I probably wouldn't care for life in the Amazon. The insects. The spiders. The diet. The lack of a daily shower. But most of all, the insects. And the spiders. So I decided to study the developing world rather than have to live in it. A moral failing I know. But the photography course was fun.

"Our teacher insisted we use large format cameras. Do you know what they are? Huge heavy boxes. We had to lug them all over Cambridge. In the summer heat and humidity. The film is a single 4X5 inch sheet you put in a frame, and then expose it. Then develop it. Then make prints. But the resolution and depth of tone is amazing. Do you know Ansel Adams, the photographer?"

Thomas shook his head.

"Google him. Or I'll send you a link. He took spectacular photographs of the American southwest. I think you'd like them. Anyway, we weren't allowed to use a normal camera until the last week of the course. I learned a lot."

"Another hidden talent."

Maggie shrugged. "More a competence than talent. And once I decided I wasn't destined for the Amazon, I really didn't do much more with it than take some family photos. Maine seascapes. Rowers on the Charles River. But I should be able to get some recognizable shots of Washfield Warham. And Grumpy," she smiled.

"And did you know the camera also does video? I can take one of Wasp moving its segments like its namesake's wings."

"Or Marsh's new Gnat. Swarming."

Maggie looked surprised.

"Beatrix told me."

"Ah yes. Nat. The G-nat." She pronounced the G. "Marsh's idea of wordplay. Although it probably wouldn't pass scrutiny at the high table, where we're held to a higher standard."

Thomas regarded his wife.

"What? Well, it wouldn't."

Maggie glared.

"Is this your obsession with my obsession? Or supposed obsession? It sounds like the title of a bad pop song."

Thomas threw up his hands, and then drained the last of his wine.

"Sorry, Papillon. Anyhow, there's a David Attenborough programme on I'd like to watch."

"All right. I'll bring the instruction manual. You can watch, I can read, and we can cuddle."

"You might want to watch as well. It's about plants and I believe it was filmed at Kew. It might give you some ideas."

"Oh. All right. I'll save the manual for the commercial breaks."

Thomas stood up and pulled out her chair.

"More wine?"

"Tempting. But I fear the manual demands a high level of sobriety."

Thomas laughed and kissed her.

"Your devotion to our gardens is touching, my dear."

Thomas, if you only knew, Maggie thought.

SUSAN ALEXANDER

Chapter 24

Crispin appeared promptly at two in an old red Vauxhall Corsa.

Maggie eyed the car.

"Is there a Ferrari engine installed under the hood?"

"No. On account that we probably won't need to make any fast getaways. And you're the one who didn't want the Porsche. And I figured instead of carrying a red rose, I'd show up in a red car. Oh, no, wait. I seem to have the rose as well."

Crispin reached down onto the seat beside him and produced a perfect, blood red rose. He handed it to Maggie.

"Um. Thank you."

"So what's the plan?"

"There's a Costa's down the road."

"I won't say I'm not disappointed..."

"Crispin!"

"All right. Hop in. Although does caffeine really rate higher with you than my own not insignificant charms?"

Maggie shook her head. She got in and for a split second worried that Crispin might hijack her to another destination. But he docilely drove to the Costa's and parked.

The coffee shop was moderately busy on a Saturday afternoon, with people taking a break from shopping. Maggie looked around carefully but saw no one she knew.

"Grab that table over there." Crispin pointed to a relatively secluded corner.

"What would you like?"

"Large cappuccino."

"Ha. I'm a triple espresso man myself."

"Que macho," said Maggie, unimpressed.

Crispin returned with their coffees.

"So what's going on with Marsh?" Maggie demanded.

"You're not going to wait until after dessert to discuss business?"

"Crispin!"

Crispin looked at her. Maggie stared back and vowed she was not going to become distracted.

She broke eye contact to take a sip of cappuccino.

"I gave Marsh a bank cheque for £5,000 to steal the Ainswick Orange from your own little secret garden at Beaumatin. With another £5,000 promised on delivery."

Maggie choked. Crispin got up and patted her on the back.

"You what?"

"I thought I'd help things along."

"But how did you…."

Crispin pulled out a tablet computer from a backpack he was carrying and opened a browser.

"Have you ever seen a satellite image of Beaumatin? All you have to do is google Beaumatin, maps and satellite."

Crispin showed her.

There was the house and the gardens. And clearly visible was the closed rectangle of the hidden plot.

"I know at some point even the rarest snowdrops have to be moved out of the greenhouse and into the ground. So I figured you had to have someplace secure and not accessible to your tourists. This was the obvious place. Are you going to tell me I was wrong?"

"No. Although I only knew about this a couple of weeks ago."

Crispin smiled smugly.

"And the Ainswick Orange?"

"Well, I noticed a certain tension any time your legendary snowdrop came up in conversation. And then the too facile segué into 'We think it was probably destroyed but maybe it's in a field someplace.'

"But if I thought a priceless snowdrop might be blooming in some adjacent field, I wouldn't wait until some hiker stumbled over it and maybe told the Ainswicks about it. If he didn't trample it. Or use a flower as a boutonnière.

"I'd hire a couple of local scout troops and have them do a grid search of every inch of land surrounding Rochford Manor. Which wasn't being done. So I figured it must have been found. And since it probably wasn't at the Manor to avoid awkward questions, I assumed it had probably been given to the Ainswicks' good friend, the 28th Baron Raynham, for safekeeping. How am I doing?"

Maggie looked down at her cappuccino and stirred the foam into the coffee. Then she looked back up at Crispin.

"I found the Ainswick Orange. After the person who had had it stolen decided it was too damning to have in her possession. After the murders. It was pretty bedraggled, although I'm not sure that's the proper botanical term. I gave it to Thomas to nurse back to health and safekeep. The Ainswicks know, of course. But no one else. Just the four of us."

Crispin grinned. "I know it's bad form to pat oneself on the back. But you must admit I'm good."

"What you are is a loose cannon. Just what is your deal with Marsh?"

"That Aunt Sarah has heard rumours that the Ainswick Orange is at Beaumatin. In a secluded plot. She's known for being fairly ruthless. And is able to pay a small fortune to get something she wants. He wasn't hard to convince."

"And you showed him the door."

"Oh. You noticed that? Anyhow, it's locked. And I'm not sure about our Nat's lock-picking skills. So he'll probably have to go over the wall."

"When?"

"Tomorrow night, I expect. I managed to put a little tracking device in that Highgrove bag he's always carrying around."

"You did?"

Crispin nodded.

"So he goes over the wall. What then?"

"Then he can be caught red-handed. Trying to steal the snowdrop. And the authorities will have a reason to take a closer look at his secret garden. At both the flowers and what else is there."

"The skeleton, you mean."

Crispin turned serious. "I think there are at least three. And those woods are no old burial plot."

"Three?"

Crispin nodded. "I told you I didn't like the place."

Maggie digested this information.

"Were you ever able to check on prescriptions? For barbiturates?"

Crispin nodded. "The Fish did. It seems Marsh's mother had a prescription. For the same kind of barbiturate that they found in Charlotte."

"So I'm not a total crackpot."

"Well, not total."

"And what you're planning. It's not entrapment?"

"I'm not a policeman."

"And your cheque?"

"A bogus account."

"You are familiar with Murphy's Law? What can go wrong will go wrong?"

"It always does. Yet here I am."

"And what if Marsh says he was just trying to satisfy his curiosity. About what rare snowdrops might be hidden at Beaumatin. And all that happens is that he's cited for trespassing. And gets a slap on the wrist.

"And what if he's caught with the Ainswick Orange? The police would love to have it. He might even claim a reward."

"You sound like my old commander."

"With good reason, I'm sure."

"Every plan needs some flexibility."

"And what are you going to do? Follow him and then leap over the wall at the critical moment and say, 'Unhand that snowdrop?'"

"I'm still considering various options."

Maggie closed her eyes. She thought of all the things that could go wrong. She thought of what Thomas would say, when he found out she was a part of this mad scheme. She thought of Charlotte. And Emily.

"Can't you trust me, Moppet?"

Maggie remained silent.

"Or would you prefer 'Let's call the whole thing off,'" he sang the line from the Cole Porter tune softly.

Maggie was reminded of Derek. She sighed.

"Very well."

"Don't worry, Moppet. No one is going to die. And you can always deny all knowledge…"

"You know I wouldn't do that."

He looked at her.

"No, I guess you wouldn't. So I'll just have to make sure nothing gets screwed up."

"That would be good."

SUSAN ALEXANDER

Chapter 25

Sunday morning Maggie went and found Thomas in his study.

"Thomas? I think I've made some progress with the camera and I wondered…"

"Yes?"

"Well, would it be possible to take some pictures…"

"The gardens are at your disposal as always, my dear."

"Yes. Of course. But I wondered…"

Thomas looked at Maggie. He leaned back and steepled his fingers.

"Just say it. Quickly. Before you get distracted," she told herself.

"I'd like to take a picture of the Beaumatin's Blondes. And the Ainswick Orange. While they're blooming."

"Are you going to send Deacon a picture so he can blog about the Ainswick Orange?"

Thomas had not been happy about Deacon's post on the Beaumatin's Blonde.

"No. Of course not. Just… for us."

Thomas shrugged.

"As you wish."

"But don't I need a key?"

"Oh. Yes. Come. I'll show you."

Thomas went to what Maggie called the mud room, where jackets, boots, hats, assorted gardening tools, and other outdoor paraphernalia were kept.

He opened a drawer in a chest Maggie seemed to recall held parts of a croquet game and badminton rackets. There was a small bowl with assorted keys.

"You know this is the key for the greenhouse."

Maggie nodded.

"This one with the tag unlocks the door."

He handed it to Maggie.

"Please remember to put it back when you're finished."

Maggie reflected on how often Thomas made her feel like she was eight years old again. Except when she was eight, she had already been too responsible to have neglected to return a key.

Thomas looked at her like he expected an assent.

"Yes, Thomas. I'll return the key."

He ruffled her curls.

"Back to admin."

"And I hope to amaze you at lunch."

Maggie took the key and the camera and the instruction manual with her and went to the door in the wall. The key worked easily.

The plot was divided into twelve rectangular beds with cement paths running between them. Among the snowdrops, Maggie identified Beaumatin's Harriet, Wasp, Diggory, EA Bowles and Green Tear as well as the Beaumatin's Blondes and the solitary Ainswick Orange.

She decided she would try to take a picture of the Ainswick Orange first. However, finding an angle that showed both the orange on the ovary and the orange on the interior segments seemed impossible until she simply lay down on the path.

"There's got to be a better way," she muttered.

Diggory, with its distinctive shape, was easier, although she still had to sit down on the ground to photograph the low flowers.

Thomas found her flat on her back trying to capture both outer and inner segments of a Beaumatin's Blonde.

He helped her up.

"They don't mention this in the manual," she remarked.

Thomas' mouth twitched.

"I believe it is common knowledge among galanthophiles that to properly see a flower, some humility is necessary. I once saw a chap who had attached a mirror to the end of a walking stick so he didn't have to squat. Given his weight, it seemed like a good solution.

"Anyhow, it's lunchtime. Mrs Cook has made a potato leek soup. A good choice for a wintry day."

Maggie had to admit it did sound good.

After lunch, Maggie told Thomas she wanted to take a few more pictures.

"Why does the image of a child with a new toy come to mind?" he teased.

"It's just that there's some sun. Who knows when that will happen again? The weather has been so foul. And we are coming to the end of the blooming season."

"I'm going to take a break and watch some cricket," Thomas announced.

"Enjoy. I'll join you in a bit and you can explain what's going on."

"Again."

"Yes. Again," she laughed. Maggie found it hard to grasp the finer points of the game.

Maggie took pictures for another hour. It was a slow process. She had brought a notebook where she recorded specifics of each shot. Exposure. Focus. Her position. Other details. Then when she looked at what she had done on a screen she would have a better idea of what worked. And what didn't.

She went to her study and uploaded the pictures onto her laptop. Then she checked on Thomas. The man had fallen asleep. No surprises here.

Maggie returned to her study and realised she had left her notebook in the garden. She needed to retrieve it.

Maggie was on edge. Crispin thought Marsh would make his attempt that evening, which made sense. Sunday was the day off at Beaumatin. If there were no houseguests, Mrs Cook left after lunch. Sometimes she would visit a cousin in Cheltenham. Otherwise she would shop. Or go to a movie. Mrs Cook liked romantic comedies. *Love Actually* seemed to be her all-time favourite. Along with *Bridget Jones* and *Notting Hill*.

After making sure the sheep were content, Ned and the men also had the day off.

Maggie returned to the garden. She took the camera, just in case there was a chance for a final shot. However, even though sunset was not until around six, clouds had gathered and the light was dimming. So no more photographs. Now where had she left that notebook?

She found the notebook beside some flourishing clumps of Green Tear. She was bending to retrieve it when she heard the door open. And close. She expected to see Thomas. But it was Marsh.

He was wearing his usual outfit of cords, jumper, a plaid shirt, boots. He had added an anorak. And he carried his Highgrove bag.

Marsh stood surveying the garden with an expression of satisfaction. He took a deep breath. He had not noticed Maggie.

Where was Crispin? He had said he was tracking the poacher.

Marsh was rummaging in his bag when he saw her.

"Well, Marsh?"

Not a line worthy of Bruce Willis or Arnold Schwarzenegger, and Mr Bond would sneer, but it would have to do.

Marsh's expressive features distorted. He kept his hand in the bag. Maggie realised Marsh was between her and the door. That wasn't good.

"I suppose it's only fair that you found our secret garden. Since I found yours."

"That was you?"

"Yes. You have our Beaumatin's Blondes. The ones that Greenaway was supposed to plant at Rochford Manor. And the Chloe Symeons. And you seem to have helped yourself to the Epsleys' snowdrop collection."

"How did you...."

"I know a lot, Marsh."

She had to keep him talking until Crispin showed up. Although this was the worst-case scenario. Marsh had not actually done anything. Except be where he shouldn't.

"I'll bet you don't know about this."

He pulled out a small jar from his bag. It was filled with a dark substance. It was hard to tell exactly what it was in the fading light.

"Apparently not. What is it?"

"Earth with a very high concentration of botrytis."

Maggie knew botrytis was a fungus that was lethal to snowdrops. And once it was in the soil, there was no treatment.

"Should I sprinkle some around in here? That would take care of your precious Beaumatin's Blondes. And Harriets. I could spread some around the rest of your gardens as well. A little of this goes a long way. But perhaps if you'd show me where the Ainswick Orange is..."

"The Ainswick Orange?" she asked while she wondered where the heck Crispin was.

"Don't play stupid. I know it's here. If you saved me some bother…"

"You'd swap the snowdrop for that jar?"

"Maybe."

"Maybe isn't good enough."

"I'll find it anyway."

"Really?"

"What do you think you can do?"

"Call the dogs."

"They won't get here before I release the botrytis."

That was true.

"All right. Put the jar down and I'll show you."

"Show me and I'll put down the jar."

Maggie wished she had a gun. But she didn't. What should she do? Stall. Keep him talking.

"What will you do with it? The Ainswick Orange? You can hardly auction it on eBay."

"A private buyer."

"A collector? Who'll plant it someplace where only he can see it and gloat?"

"That's not your problem. This is." He brandished the jar.

Maggie briefly wondered if Marsh's threat about the botrytis was a hoax, like the security in his secret garden. But realised she couldn't take a chance.

"Now show me." Marsh was impatient.

"All right. It's over here somewhere."

She moved towards the far end of the plot. Marsh was following her when the door pushed open again. Maggie expected Crispin, but it was Thomas.

"Maggie?"

"Thomas! Watch out!"

Marsh whirled around.

"Marsh? What the hell…"

With his free hand, Marsh reached in his bag and pulled out a knife. A carving knife. Wicked looking.

Then, without warning, Marsh rushed at Thomas. Thomas reflexively put up his arm to defend himself. The blade sank into his upper bicep.

"Argh!"

Thomas staggered back, holding his bleeding arm.

"Thomas!" Maggie started towards her husband.

Marsh looked at the jar. Calmly and deliberately, he tossed it towards the plot where the Beaumatin's Blondes were planted.

Maggie leapt and, in a save worthy of a Premier League goalkeeper, caught the jar.

She carefully put the jar down on the pathway and scrambled back up to face Marsh.

But he was distracted by another arrival.

"Marsh!"

Crispin was perched on top of the wall. He jumped down onto the clusters of Wasps.

"Be careful! He has a knife," Maggie warned.

Marsh sprang at Crispin. The men grappled, then Crispin cried out and staggered back, his hands against his abdomen.

Maggie grabbed her camera and ran at Marsh. She swung the camera by its strap as hard as she could and it slammed into his face. She could hear cartilage crunch.

Marsh howled and dropped the knife.

Maggie bent to pick it up and Marsh stomped down hard on her arm, his hands held against his shattered nose.

"Ah!"

She mustn't let Marsh get the knife, was all she thought.

He stomped again. And again.

"Stupid bitch!"

Maggie rammed her shoulder into his hip and he staggered back.

Marsh kicked out at Maggie, who tumbled onto the path. He grabbed a handful of her hair and pulled her up.

A stranger came through the garden door.

"Fish. Help her," called Crispin.

The Fish pulled out a Glock pistol.

"It's over, Marsh. Let her go."

Marsh faced the newcomer. The Fish was slight, of medium height and dressed all in black. He had dark hair and dark eyes and his thin face was acne scarred.

Marsh wrapped an arm around Maggie's neck.

"Throw away the gun or I'll break her neck."

"Left ear or right?" was The Fish's calm reply.

"What?"

"Left, then."

And The Fish let off a round. It blew off the top part of Marsh's left ear. Marsh shrieked and let go of Maggie.

Maggie admired the shot. She assumed The Fish had hit his target. At least she hoped it was Marsh's ear at which he had been aiming.

"Kneel! Hands behind your head," ordered Fish.

Maggie rushed to Thomas. He was holding his arm. It was bleeding but not severely. It seemed that no arteries had been severed.

"Will you be all right while I…"

Thomas grunted.

Maggie hurried to Crispin. He was lying on his back in the midst of the Wasps. He was holding his side to try to stem the bleeding.

"Crispin? I'm calling for help."

"Tim. *2," he managed.

"I'll call him, Crisps," said The Fish, who had bound Marsh's hands behind him with a large plastic bag tie he had pulled from a pocket.

Maggie ripped off her jacket and held it against Crispin's wound.

"Crispin, you said no one was going to die. So don't."

"If you say so, Moppet."

Maggie called Inspector Willis. She was relieved when he answered.

"Um, Inspector Willis? It's Maggie. Eliot. Er, Raynham. There's... Nat Marsh has stabbed Thomas and... someone else. Can you please come? To Beaumatin? And make sure an ambulance is on the way. Maybe two. No. No one is dead. But people are hurt. Badly hurt. So hurry would be good."

The Fish was examining Crispin's wound.

"Hang in there, Crisps. I don't think this is the one that'll do for you."

Thomas pushed himself off the wall that he had been leaning against and lurched over to Crispin.

"Good God. Archibald-Atherton?"

"And who the hell are you?" he demanded of The Fish.

"Name's Pilchard. Fred Pilchard. But you can call me Fish."

"Fish? Right. And you, Marsh."

Thomas pushed the man over with his foot. Marsh landed on his wounded ear.

"Ow," he howled.

"You're lucky the dogs are in the house."

Maggie was kneeling by Crispin again.

"He's losing too much blood. He should... we need blankets."

"I'll go," offered The Fish.

"No, you don't know where. And the dogs... Let me. Thomas will you be all right? Help is coming."

Maggie sprinted to the house, grabbed some blankets and towels, and ran back.

While she put a clean towel against his wound and wrapped a blanket around Crispin, she asked The Fish in a low voice, "Did you get Tim?"

He nodded. "I expect black helicopters at any moment."

Sirens could be heard in the distance.

"I'll go tell them where..." Thomas said and went off.

Maggie knelt beside Crispin. She put his head in her lap and held his hand.

"No grapes?"

"Hush."

"Tim is going to be pissed.

"Tim is going to give you a medal, if I have anything to say about it."

"I'd settle for a red rose…"

Medics appeared. Maggie hoped Thomas was being treated.

"Fish, can you get people out of here and see that they're… someplace else?"

"Sure thing."

"But before you go…"

Maggie lowered her voice. "Crispin said he'd put a tracking thing in Marsh's bag. Could you…."

The Fish became all business.

"You people. Move him. Carefully. It's no good him lying here in the dirt," The Fish ordered.

"And you. You're coming with me." Pilchard grabbed Marsh by the back of his jacket, hauled him up and marched him through the door with one hand. With his other hand he grabbed the Highgrove bag.

The medics lifted Crispin onto a stretcher and also left.

Maggie was aware that Marsh had hurt her arm when he'd stomped on it, but it felt numb, not sore. Another effect of adrenaline, she told herself. Meanwhile, she knew there were two things she had to do. And quickly. Before the police arrived.

First she ran to the greenhouse, grabbed a pot and a trowel, returned and dug up the Ainswick Orange. Her right hand didn't seem to be working, so she used her left.

"You are more trouble than you're worth," she scolded the snowdrop.

She filled in the hole, smoothed the soil, and then hid the plant in the greenhouse on a bottom shelf behind an assortment of empty pots.

She made one last trip back to the secret garden. She found the jar of botrytis—she saw no reason not to believe Marsh—and shuddered. She used a handkerchief to carefully pick it up, and then wrapped it in her blood-stained jacket that was lying by the Wasps. She dashed back to the house and put the whole in an empty bin in the trash room. It was not a lead-lined container, but it would have to do.

Maggie found one of the ambulances just pulling away. She assumed it carried Crispin, as Thomas was sitting in the back of the other.

"Thomas?"

A medic was wrapping a bandage around his arm.

"They want me to go to the hospital."

"Then you should. I'll call William. And I should probably wait and talk to the police."

"Willis?"

Maggie nodded. Thomas didn't like Willis. And the feeling was mutual.

"I'll come as soon as I can."

"Or I'll have William bring me home. I don't think they'll keep me."

He paused and gave Maggie a grim look.

"Plus I'll be interested in hearing just what you know about… all this."

Thomas' tone was neutral but she could tell he was angry.

"Yes. And I'll be very happy to tell you what I know," she replied, equally neutral.

Three police cars raced up the drive. The medic had Thomas lie down and strapped him in. The doors were closed and the ambulance took off.

Willis got out of the first car, followed by Detective Sergeant Patrick. Willis was in his late forties, Maggie's height, with greying brown hair and hooded grey eyes. He looked perpetually tired and his suits typically looked like they needed pressing. Patrick was twenty years' Willis' junior and made up in fashion sense what Willis lacked, with a preference for body hugging suits and dark shirts.

"Maggie. What happened? You said there were no dead bodies. I hope that's still the case."

"It is as long as Lennox Archibald-Atherton survives his wound. Nat Marsh stabbed him. And stabbed Lord Raynham. While Marsh was trying to steal a snowdrop."

Willis looked dumbfounded. Then he noticed The Fish. The agent was standing guard over Marsh, who was sitting on Beaumatin's front steps. Marsh's ear was still bleeding profusely and his nose was crooked and bloody. He was already developing two black eyes.

"And who's this?" he indicated Pilchard.

The Fish pulled a small leather case out of an interior jacket pocket, flipped it open and showed his identification to Willis.

Willis looked even more dumbfounded. He recovered and said, "All right. Constables, take this man into custody." He indicated Marsh.

"And we'll need a statement from you. And contact info," he told The Fish.

Then he noticed Maggie was unconsciously holding her arm across her stomach.

"Maggie! What happened to your arm?"

Maggie looked down. Her wrist and hand had swollen to the size of a grapefruit. Possibly a cantaloupe. She hadn't been aware of it.

She shrugged.

"Marsh stomped on it when we were struggling for his knife."

"His knife?" Willis scowled.

"Then you'd also better go…" He looked around. The ambulance and medics had left.

"I'll take you. You can tell me what happened on the way. Patrick, the SOCOs…"

Willis turned back to Maggie.

"Where did this happen, exactly?"

Oh dear.

"I'll show you. But I need your promise the SOCOs won't trample the plants. That Sergeant Patrick will make sure…"

"I can't guarantee something like that."

"Then I'll stay here and make sure they're careful. And not say anything until William Conyers is here. Which won't be soon because I expect he's with Thomas. And even then I am sure he will advise me not to provide… certain information. Which you would probably want to have."

The Fish grinned. "You tell 'im, Lady Raynham."

"And I probably shouldn't say anything anyway until I have spoken with Mr Pilchard's superior. Unless of course I can be sure the plants…"

Willis remembered Lord Raynham had referred to his wife as pig-headed. He was beginning to appreciate what he meant.

"How about you show me the, uh, crime scene."

It was getting dark. Maggie led them through the gardens and through the door into the walled garden.

"Please keep to the paths," she urged.

"It all happened here. There should be a knife. On the path. Oh, here it is. And my camera. I, er, hit Marsh with it. When I was afraid he was going to stab Crispin, er, Lennox Archibald-Atherton again. Oh dear."

It was broken. Smashed. Beyond repair. Maggie was glad she hadn't returned the spare camera yet.

"I believe Mr Pilchard took Marsh's Highgrove bag. The one he uses for his snowdrop poaching. He was also carrying the knife in there. As you can see, everything else is on the cement, except here where Cris..., er, Archibald-Atherton fell. I'm sure there's blood. Those are Wasps. The snowdrops. But can you please promise..."

Maggie began to feel strange. Woozy. Nauseous. Her arm was throbbing.

"I'm sorry." She sat down on the ground abruptly, just missing the clusters of Ethel Merton.

"Maggie?"

Maggie was shivering.

"I think she may be in shock, sir," said Patrick.

"Maggie. We need to get you to a hospital," said a worried Willis.

"No. Not until you promise. You can't force me," she said through chattering teeth.

An exasperated Willis glanced at Patrick.

"Jack, can you make sure?"

"Yes, sir. Lady Raynham, I'll see that the SOCOs don't trample the flowers."

"Thank you. It's particularly important for the Blondes. They're over there," she pointed. "And nothing happened anywhere near there."

"The Blondes," repeated Patrick.

"And ask Mrs Cook to call me please. I have something important to tell her."

"Yes, I'm sure you do," said Willis, humouring Maggie.

"And be careful of the dogs. They're in the house. They won't realise you're police."

That Willis did believe.

"Tell everyone to avoid the house, Patrick."

"Yes, sir," said his sergeant with feeling.

SUSAN ALEXANDER

Chapter 26

Maggie was subdued on the ride to the hospital and Willis concentrated on driving on the single-track lane in the dark.

She had stopped shivering. Now her arm and wrist just hurt. Really hurt. She suspected a bone had been broken. That would be boring. She had never had a broken bone.

Maggie wondered what she should say. What she could say. She wished she could talk to Crispin. Well, she just hoped Crispin was all right. She would have to see. Should she talk to Tim? Not until she knew whether anything she said would get Crispin into trouble. And that they were telling Tim the same story. Maybe The Fish… But she didn't know what Pilchard knew and was fairly sure he would be long gone by the time she returned to Beaumatin.

William then. She trusted William. And anything she said to him was confidential. She would tell him the whole story. See what he thought.

And that left Thomas. She knew he would be furious. Even though she had been proven right about Marsh. At least about him being a bad guy. And about the murders? Well certainly after today they could search Marsh's house. And his secret garden. Find those graves Crispin believed were there. She could tell Willis about that without involving Crispin. At worst they would charge her with trespassing. Give her a slap on the wrist. And if it were broken and in a cast, that would be…

Willis parked in the emergency zone, came around and opened the door. He helped Maggie out and walked her into the A&E. She seemed dazed and was covered with

Crispin's blood from head to foot. He settled her in the nearest available chair.

People stared.

Willis spotted Raynham with his arm in a sling. He was standing with William Conyers.

The men eyed each other.

"Lady Raynham is injured. I think her arm is badly broken. She's possibly in shock as well. She should see a doctor. Rather urgently."

Thomas' mouth formed a thin line.

"Indeed."

Both Willis and William stared at him.

William said, "I'll go see if Giles…" Giles Sumner was a surgeon at the hospital and a friend of the barrister.

"And Lord Raynham, as long as we're here, and I assume you'll want to wait for Lady Raynham, I'd appreciate a statement."

Thomas nodded curtly. "Although I'm not sure there's much I can tell you."

William returned with Giles Sumner.

"Where is she?"

"Over here."

Thomas had not seen Maggie. She was sitting hunched in a chair holding her arm across her middle. Her swollen wrist looked dire, but more shocking was the blood that covered her clothes and was smeared on her face. And in her hair, which looked like it had been through a cyclone.

"Maggie!"

It took Maggie a moment to recognise her husband.

"Thomas?"

She noticed the sling. "Oh. Your arm. How are you?"

"I'm fine. But you…" he said gruffly.

"Giles is going to take care of you. Giles?"

Giles looked shocked when he saw Maggie, then became all business. He motioned a nurse forward who pushed a wheel chair. They helped Maggie into it."

"She'll need x-rays. Possibly… I'll let you know as soon as I can."

The nurse wheeled Maggie away.

"So, Lord Raynham. Mr Conyers, you're welcome to sit in too, of course," said Willis.

Father and son followed the detective into the canteen where they ordered coffee.

Once they were seated, Willis repeated, "So, Lord Raynham. All Lady Raynham could tell me, well, she showed me where Marsh's attack occurred. And pointed out his knife. Where it had fallen. And her camera. But wouldn't say more until I promised your snowdrops would come to no harm from the SOCOs. I've left Sergeant Patrick at the scene to make sure that happens. Or doesn't happen."

Thomas shook his head.

"I'm not sure how much I can tell you. I was watching the cricket. Fell asleep. Woke up. Realised Lady Raynham was not in the house. Remembered she'd been taking pictures in the part of the garden where our rarest, most valuable plants are kept.

"I went to see if she were still there. It was getting dark. I found her with Marsh. He came at me. With a knife. Vicious thing. No warning. Stabbed me. As you can see," he indicated his sling.

"Then young Archibald-Atherton came along. I have no idea why. What he was doing there. He'd visited the gardens Friday. Part of a seminar group from Rochford Manor. Archibald-Atherton told me he was standing in for his aunt, Lady Sarah Archibald-Atherton. Who had a touch of sciatica. Or perhaps it was lumbago. Anyway, Marsh was there with the group as well. I did notice them talking. But what either Marsh or Archibald-Atherton was up to, I really don't know.

"I was at school with his father. Understood young Lennox had had a distinguished military career and was now in some ministry or other. Lady Raynham seemed to know him. Well, he and Lady Sarah had been at our table at a do in London on the 22nd. I know they talked then. Apparently they had common acquaintances in Oxford."

Keeping the baronial eye on the wife as usual, thought Willis. And save me from all these toffs... Things always got complicated when titles were involved.

"So Archibald-Atherton..."

"Oh yes. Well, Marsh rushed at him. Stabbed him. Got him in the gut. Rather worse than me. Then... hmm. I think somehow Lady Raynham managed to get Marsh to drop the knife. And then some other fellow... Strange chap. Seemed to know Archibald-Atherton. He, er, subdued Marsh. Shot him. You were called. And the emergency services."

Thomas paused.

"But I got the impression... Well, that I was coming in in the middle of things. With Lady Raynham and Marsh. And you know about Lady Raynham and Marsh."

"Um. What is it you think I know about Lady Raynham and Marsh, Lord Raynham?" Willis was careful to use her title.

"This obsession of hers. About Marsh. His being involved in those deaths last summer. And the suicide of Charlotte Verney. I had thought... Well, she'd convinced me she was, er, over it. That she had moved on. In fact she accused me of being obsessed about her obsession."

Thomas smiled grimly.

"And while Marsh is... well, he's certainly no gent. Has a bit of a dodgy reputation in fact. In the galanthophile community. Thought to be a poacher, given the chance. Not that anything's been proven.

"As I said, he was in the part of our garden that has our most valuable plants..." Thomas paused as he remembered the Ainswick Orange.

"So perhaps he had come to poach. But why he would have attacked me? With a knife? Over something that would have meant embarrassment certainly. Perhaps some people who would no longer deal with him. But more than that? I'm mystified, quite frankly."

Susan Alexander

Chapter 27

Thomas and William went to see if Giles Sumner had any news of Maggie.

"Several bones in her wrist are broken. And she has a severe fracture of her ulna. Displaced. Bone almost poked through the skin. I gather the bloke that stabbed you stomped on her arm. With his boot. More than once."

The men tried not to wince.

"She was trying to keep him from getting his knife back, I believe. Anyway, she'll need an operation to reset her ulna. Pins. Can't do much about her wrist until that's set. That will be tomorrow morning. We'll have our best man on it. Meanwhile, she's been given painkillers. A mild sedative. And an IV. She was in shock."

The men thanked the surgeon and hurried off to see Maggie.

Maggie looked wan and somewhat lost. Her arm from shoulder to hand was encased in a fiberglass cast and an IV dripped liquid into a vein.

"Thomas. Are you all right?" She indicated his sling.

He shrugged. "Tiresome. But it could be worse."

Maggie nodded. Then, "I'm not allowed any liquids after midnight. Because of the operation. But I wondered... could you get me a cup of coffee please? I'd... I'd just feel better, I think. And the nurse said there was no reason I couldn't."

"Of course, my dear. I'll be right back."

As soon as Thomas left, Maggie said to William, "I really need to talk to you. The situation is rather complicated. Quite complicated. But other people are involved and I don't want to say anything to Inspector Willis until… well at least until we've talked and I know… Can you put Willis off until I've had a chance… And I'm afraid your father will be cranky about it. Not that…

"I'm sorry. They've given me all these drugs…

"But there is one thing. Could you please find out about Lennox? Archibald-Atherton? I think they brought him here. How he is? And perhaps where he is? His room number? Unless Tim…"

"Who?"

"No one. Just if you could please find out. I'd be very grateful."

William went to the nurse's station, had a brief conversation and then returned.

"Mr Archibald Atherton is in serious but stable condition. They operated and hopefully repaired all the damage from, um, Marsh's attack. He'll need to recuperate. And he's three doors down the hall from you here."

Maggie looked relieved. Thomas came in with three cups of coffee.

"Thank you."

"I'm sure you'd like to talk," William said. He took a coffee and excused himself.

As soon as he left, Maggie said, "Thomas. I have to tell you. I removed the Ainswick Orange from the garden. It's in a pot in the greenhouse. Behind some spare pots on a bottom shelf. I thought it was best if the police were going to be, um, going to be looking around. I hope I didn't stress it too much.

"And, maybe even more important. Before you came. Marsh had a jar. He said it was full of soil that had botrytis. And he threatened to toss it all around the garden. The, uh, walled garden. Unless I showed him where the Ainswick Orange was.

"I was trying to stall him. When you came. When he attacked you, I, er, managed to stop it from getting out of the jar. The botrytis. And I wrapped up the jar in my jacket and put it in one of the bins in the house. But you need to warn Mrs Cook. It would be terrible if…"

Maggie's eyes filled with tears.

"I'm sorry. It's just so…"

Thomas felt his anger at what he felt was her deceit ebb. He would put his questions aside for now.

He kissed her forehead. "Mon pauvre papillon. I'll come see you tomorrow morning after they fix your arm."

Maggie attempted a smile. She closed her eyes. Thomas left.

Maggie dozed, then realised there was something she still had to do. She slipped out of bed and, wheeling the IV stand, peeked out the door. Down the hall, at the nurses' station, one of the nurses was talking on a telephone. The other was checking bottles in a medicine cabinet.

Maggie hurried down the hall in the other direction, carrying the IV stand so it didn't make any noise. One door. Two. Three. She quietly pushed it open.

In the dim light, she saw a familiar figure in a bed.

"Crispin? Lennox?" she whispered.

There was no response. He was asleep.

She crept closer to the bed. He looked pale. Boyish. He also had tubes going in and out. At least he would recover. Given time. She was terribly thankful for that.

Maggie leaned over and kissed him gently on the forehead. She was rising when fingers wrapped in her hair and she was pulled back down and kissed properly.

Crispin grinned.

"Hello, my Moppet. What brings you to my bedside? Besides my obvious charms."

"I wanted to make sure you were all right. I was worried. But I see I needn't have been," she finished.

Crispin noticed Maggie's IV stand and the tube that ran into her arm. And her cast. And her hospital gown.

"What? You're in here too? Why?"

"Right down the hall. Three doors."

"Yes. That's nice. Convenient except for all these tubes. But that doesn't answer my question. What's that for?" he indicated the cast.

Maggie sighed. "I was trying to get Marsh's knife and he, er, stomped on my arm. Broke some bones. They're operating to pin them back together tomorrow."

Crispin winced.

"Oh. But more important. Willis. Whom you call my tame inspector except really he's not. Tame. He wants to talk to me. About what happened. I've asked Thomas' son William, he's a barrister, to put him off. Because I didn't want to say anything until I checked with you. About what to say.

"I can say I think Marsh was at Beaumatin to poach some snowdrops. I've hidden the Ainswick Orange, by the way. But I'm not sure I can explain why you were there. Let alone Mr Fish. Er, Pilchard. And as for everything else. Marsh's own garden. The bones. The murders. Charlotte. I just don't know. And I don't want to get you into trouble with the police. Or with Tim. I assume he'll also want some explanations."

Crispin grimaced at the mention of Tim.

"Yes. He probably would have preferred for me to keep a lower profile."

"I would imagine."

Crispin thought.

"When are they… putting in your pins?"

"Tomorrow morning first thing, I expect."

"Then let's talk after that."

"Tim won't send black helicopters in the night to spirit you off to some secret location?"

"Unlikely. They've eliminated most of the black helicopters since the budget cuts."

Maggie smiled. "And Thomas said he would be here after the operation. Just so… Well, I'm sure he's also wondering what you were doing. What we were doing."

"Yes. Murphy certainly seems to have had his revenge."

"He generally does."

"One way or the other, we'll talk tomorrow. Don't say anything until we do."

Maggie nodded.

Crispin was holding her hand. He raised it to his lips and kissed it.

"Damn these tubes. They certainly limit... possibilities. But. Three doors away, did you say?"

"Well, I'm glad you're all right," said Maggie tartly and sneaked back to her room.

She opened her door to find Inspector Willis standing by her bed, in confrontation with a nurse. Both stared at her.

"Lady Raynham. You're not supposed to be out of bed," said the nurse sternly.

"I'm so sorry." Maggie was meek. "I just really needed to, er, stretch my legs. I didn't mean to cause any upset."

"Humpf."

"Would it be all right if I had a word?" asked Willis,

"Of course," said Maggie.

"Five minutes," the nurse said severely as she left.

Maggie and Willis looked at each other.

"Do you know how Sergeant Patrick managed with your SOCOs?" Maggie asked.

"I'm assuming no news is good news."

"I hope so."

There was a pause.

"Maggie, I assume there is more to this than an attempt to steal a rare snowdrop."

Maggie thought about what she could say.

"Yes."

"Then what is it?"

Maggie hesitated.

"The truth. Not one of your, er, performances."

"All right. Inspector Willis. Tom. In the past I know I have withheld information. And pretended that I hadn't. But only when I had a good reason to do so.

"So this time, I will tell you directly that I can't talk to you right now. Not if I'm going to be, er, forthcoming. But only for a few more hours. Then I'll tell you everything."

Willis scowled.

"Is it about Walker? And Greenaway?"

"Yes, but there's more."

"More?"

"Yes. More. But there is one thing I can tell you. Under no circumstances can you release Marsh. At least until we've talked. Can you promise you'll keep him in custody until, say, this time tomorrow at the latest?"

"You want me to keep a man in custody based on… what? I'm sure his solicitor is trying to get him bailed as we speak."

"After he stabbed two people? And broke my arm? You must be joking."

Willis looked into indignant green eyes.

He sighed.

"All right. Until this time tomorrow. But if you don't tell me everything. Everything. I'll have you up on charges for obstructing an investigation. Are we clear?"

"Clear. And thank you."

Maggie reflexively extended her hand. Even with the drugs, the pain was breath taking. She closed her eyes. Swayed.

"Maggie?"

Willis steadied her.

"You need to get into bed."

She nodded.

He held her tubes as she climbed in. He adjusted the pillow under her head and pulled the bedcovers over her. He would have liked to have smoothed her hair, but…

Instead he said, "Until tomorrow, then."

He left. And as she drifted off to sleep, Maggie reflected that tomorrow was going to be a very full day indeed.

SUSAN ALEXANDER

Chapter 28

Maggie woke up back in her room to find Thomas sitting beside her bed.

Water, please," she croaked.

Thomas held a glass for her and she took several sips.

"Thank you."

"How do you feel?"

"Numb. It's the great thing about anaesthesia."

She looked at her arm and hand, wrapped in a cast that extended above her elbow.

"Were all the King's horses and all the King's men able to put Humpty Dumpty together again?"

"So I'm told. Assuming you don't do anything to disarrange things while you heal."

"Did your source say how long that would take?"

"Given the severity of the breaks? Possibly as long as two months."

"Two months? But what am I going to do?"

"I imagine you will have to learn to use your left hand. And use your keyboard one-handed."

"Yes, but…"

"And I also imagine you will be spending some time with Inspector Willis."

Maggie noticed a certain frostiness in Thomas' tone.

"Thomas, are you angry?"

"Angry? Why would you think I'd be angry?"

"Well, being invaded by a snowdrop poacher and being stabbed might make you angry."

"Quite."

"But you're also angry at me, I think."

Thomas' mouth set in a thin line.

"About Marsh."

Maggie felt the temperature in the room plummet.

"You led me to believe you had abandoned your… crusade against Marsh. You even accused me of being obsessed about it."

"Yes. I know."

Thomas fumed.

"Does it make a difference that Marsh really is a bad man?"

Silence.

"How is your arm?"

"It hurts. And is also inconvenient."

"No riding. No driving. And I imagine you are also having to use a keyboard with one hand. How hard is that with your spreadsheets?"

"Humpf."

"Did you check on the Ainswick Orange?"

"Yes."

"Is it all right?"

"Well enough."

"Good. I'm glad."

Silence.

"And was much damage done to the other snowdrops?"

"The Wasps were crushed. And bloody. But the bulbs were not damaged. Otherwise none."

"Then I must thank Sergeant Patrick."

Silence.

"And did you find Marsh's jar? In the bin?"

"Yes. Although for all I could tell it might have contained coffee grounds. I gave it to the forensic people who will have it tested. If they have the budget for it."

"I'm just relieved it's not at Beaumatin."

Silence.

"Thomas…"

"William said he would be in to see you shortly. That you needed to talk to him."

"Yes."

"Before you talked to Willis."

"Yes."

"So I assume there is more to this than Marsh's snowdrop poaching."

"Yes."

"And it involves Lennox Archibald-Atherton. And that Fish person,"

Now it was Maggie's turn to be silent.

Thomas glared.

"Thomas. I would just love to have a knockdown, drag-out fight with you about all this. But not here. And not now. When I've just…"

Maggie lifted her arm in its cast and then winced.

"And it's… complicated. Which is why I need to talk to William. But I will tell you everything…" Well almost everything Maggie added to herself.

"I expect later today or at worst tomorrow. But for now… Just… If you could please…."

Thomas's frost thawed slightly.

"Papillon. I hold to my original opinion that you are pig-headed. And a crackpot. And I do expect you to tell me everything. A full confession. Then… I expect I may forgive you. Maybe. Given that you have certainly forgiven me… But.no promises. We will have to see."

Thomas leaned over and kissed his wife. And kissed her again. Sighed.

"I will wait and let you talk to William," he said finally and left.

William came in a few minutes later carrying two containers of coffee.

"I thought you might like this."

"Thank you."

"How are you?"

"Wishing I were someplace else."

"I imagine."

"And neither your father nor I will be able to ride or drive or do most things requiring two hands for some time. Which will make your father extremely cranky, I expect. And he's already extremely cranky."

"About Marsh."

"Yes."

"So you were going to tell me about it?"

"Yes. Although there's quite a lot to tell."

"Then it's good that we have coffee."

So Maggie began. With Charlotte's suicide.

"I could never believe that Charlotte would kill herself. She was so totally devoted to Emily. Although she certainly had developed a… a crush on Nick Greenaway. So even if I were wrong, about the suicide, I was sure she would never have killed herself like that. Where Emily could have found her. As she did."

William nodded. "I found that hard to understand myself."

Maggie went on to tell William about the missing snowdrops. And the deaths of Walker and Greenaway and her suspicion that Marsh was somehow involved.

"But even Inspector Willis was convinced by the obvious solution. Your father wouldn't listen and accused me of being obsessed…"

William, who knew his father, grimaced.

"And with everything else that was going on, I let it drop. Until it was snowdrop season again. And Beatrix brought Marsh to Beaumatin.

"So knowing I could expect no support from Willis or your father, I called an old friend who works in the government. And asked for his help. I thought if I were correct in any of my suspicions, Marsh would have the Beaumatin's Blondes that Greenaway took in his famous secret garden. Which was rumoured to be protected by vicious dogs. Laser alarms. Retinal scanners. Motion detectors. Intimidating stuff. I asked my friend if he knew someone who could, um, assess the situation and help me get in."

William looked gobsmacked.

"This friend. Does he work for MI6?"

Maggie shrugged.

"Classified."

She paused.

"Anyhow… The someone with whom he, um, connected me turned out to be, um, Lennox Archibald-Atherton."

"Lennox Archibald-Atherton?" William looked even more flabbergasted.

Maggie nodded.

"And we found Marsh's secret garden and the Beaumatin's Blondes were indeed there. As well as the Epsleys' snowdrop collection."

She told William about Marsh's last minute absence and the theft during the ball.

"And then we found the bones. Or I found the bones."

"Bones?"

Maggie told William about the bones and Archibald-Atherton's belief that there were more bodies buried in the garden.

"Good God."

"And it would have been awkward to go to the police."

"Yes. It certainly would."

"So Crispin, um, Archibald-Atherton came up with a scheme to pay Marsh to steal the Ainswick Orange."

"But the Ainswick Orange was stolen."

"Yes. But the rumour is it may still be, um, around. And Archi-, oh, Lennox convinced Marsh it was in Beaumatin's own secret garden. You know about that, I assume. The walled garden."

"Yes."

"Lennox thought if Marsh were caught red-handed trying to poach snowdrops at Beaumatin, the police could search his house. And his garden. I had my doubts and of course it all went horribly wrong, but at least the police now have Marsh in custody. They do still have him in custody?" She asked worriedly.

"Yes."

"And so they have an excuse to do a search."

William regarded Maggie.

"But my problem is..."

"You think you have only one problem?"

"Well, I think Lennox may have, um, exceeded his briefing. And I don't want to get him into trouble. And I did kind of trespass when I went exploring Marsh's garden. And there's also The Fish. Er, a man named Fred Pilchard. Or at least that's what I'm told his name is. He's a colleague of Lennox and he also got involved and I don't want him to get into difficulties because of all this either.

"And although I don't think luring Marsh to Beaumatin qualifies as entrapment, still, he could argue... Anyway I wanted to tell you everything before I even considered talking to Willis. And I still need to talk to Lennox. Who is conveniently down the hall. Unless Tim has had him spirited away..."

"Tim?"

"My, er, friend in the government."

William was speechless, which was a rare state for a barrister.

"And I know it seems that I may have been foolish. But Emily, William. If I were right, to be able to tell her that her mother would never have left her willingly. Never have acted so that Emily would find her like that."

William nodded. He thought.

"Well, I will certainly need to be there when you talk to Willis. As for your, um, friends from the government, I'm at a loss. Those sorts of, er, hijinks are beyond my experience. But you want to be very careful not to be charged with obstructing an investigation."

"I know. Willis already threatened me with that."

"He did? Well, that's not good, then."

Maggie sighed.

"I need to get my father back to Beaumatin. I am sure Mrs Cook will look after him. And I'm needed at court. I will contact Willis and arrange a time for an interview. I gather you will be here until tomorrow?"

"That's what I understand."

"Perhaps I can convince Willis to see you once you're back at Beaumatin."

"That would be fine except apparently there are issues about holding Marsh. And I'm afraid if he's released he would go destroy whatever is in his secret garden. And his home. That could be incriminating. And then it would all have been for nothing."

"But he stabbed two people. Assaulted you."

Maggie shrugged.

"Well, at least don't talk to Willis unless I am here. I am free later this afternoon. You can call me."

"All right."

William left. Not even a minute later, Lennox came in. He was in a wheelchair. The wheelchair was being pushed by Tim.

Tim glared at Maggie.

"Well, here's another nice mess you've gotten me into!" he said.

"Hardy. From Laurel and Hardy. And I don't recall ever getting you into any previous messes."

"Well, it certainly feels like it," Tim snapped.

Maggie glanced at Crispin/Lennox, who was avoiding making eye contact.

"And you had to go and drag The Fish into it as well."

Lennox now was looking at the floor. Apparently he found the pattern in the linoleum interesting.

"All right, Tim. Mea culpa. Entirely mea culpa. I take full responsibility. And have refused to say a word to Inspector Willis until we—or as I had expected—Lennox and I--had had a chance to talk. So I would not say anything… indiscrete."

At this Crispin/Lennox looked up.

"It was not your fault. I was the one who…"

"Oh be quiet," Tim snapped. "So it's like that, is it? I should have known. Anyway, I've heard what Lennox had to say. Now I want to hear your side of things."

Maggie was exhausted and her arm hurt and she would have loved another cup of coffee. But figured it would not be a good idea to ask.

A nurse peaked in with some pills in a paper cup and was surprised to see Tim and Lennox.

Tim grabbed the pills.

"I'll see that Lady Raynham takes those. Now please make sure that we're not disturbed," he barked.

The nurse began to retreat.

"No. Wait. Are some of those for this fellow here?"

The nurse looked. "For Mr Archibald-Atherton? Yes, sir."

"Then I'll take those too."

The nurse obediently handed over a cup, which Tim passed to Lennox.

He handed Maggie her cup, tried to give her the water glass, and then noticed her cast.

"Humpf."

She took the pills, and then some water.

"So. Begin."

"Some of this you've heard…"

"Yes. But remind me anyway."

So Maggie began again with Charlotte's supposed suicide and ended with Marsh's attack in the Beaumatin garden. Needless to say, she omitted certain… events. As

Crispin had said, what happens in the caravan, stays in the caravan.

When she was finished, Tim said, "Humpf. Yes. It seems this Marsh is even worse than you thought. If Lennox here is correct. And as, despite his numerous failings, I see no reason to doubt the accuracy of his eyesight, I would assume he is. So here's what we're going to do.

"I have called in Scotland Yard. Someone whom you know, I believe. They have better forensic people as well as a decent forensic anthropologist, whom it looks like we're going to need. Willis won't be happy, but tough tuna, as you like to say. Given my department's considerable investment in this debacle already, I don't want the formal investigation bollocked up.

"DCI Dexter and Willis will interview both of you together. While I am present. And if anything arises that I consider to be problematic, I will simply say it is classified. Much better than some solicitor whinging on about his client not answering some question, I'm sure you'd agree.

"And Dexter can also sort out your husband, while he's about it. I gather his lordship is somewhat grumpy at the moment?"

Maggie wondered for an instant if Tim had bugged her room. Then she decided she would stop worrying about what Tim knew. Since apparently neither she nor Lennox were going to be thrown to the lions. Or at least she hoped not.

"Grumpy. Yes," Maggie agreed.

"Let me see if Dexter has arrived. And Willis. I assume I can leave you two alone together for a few minutes?"

He left before either could think of a suitable reply.

Maggie and Crispin looked at each other.

"How are you?" Crispin asked.

"I hope one of those pills was for pain. You?"

"Same here."

"Any news of Pilchard?"

"I think The Fish has swum safely back out to sea and any questions about him will certainly be... classified." Crispin grinned.

"And Tim seems like he would prefer to keep us out of jail. Although did we really do anything illegal? Aside from some trespassing?"

"You don't think tracking Marsh's car electronically was legal?" Crispin demanded.

"Oh. I had forgotten about that."

"You should probably continue to do so."

"Do you think they'll get him? Marsh?"

"Since Tim called in Dexter. He wouldn't have done that unless he was reasonably convinced. And those bones. And, what looks like to my experienced eye, those other graves. And Marsh had to have known they were there."

Crispin glanced at the door, which was firmly closed. He gingerly got out of the wheelchair and walked carefully over to Maggie. Then he leaned over and kissed her.

"Irresistible," he said as he walked back and lowered himself into the wheelchair. "And..."

He never got to finish what he had been about to say, as the door opened and Tim returned, followed by Dexter and a very unhappy-looking Willis.

"Thomas is not the only one who is grumpy," Maggie thought.

Tim looked around the room.

"I think we could use two more chairs. There are some in Archibald-Atherton's room. Dexter?"

The moment the men left, Maggie said, "Inspector Willis?"

She figured whatever she had to say could be said in front of Crispin.

Willis looked at her sourly.

"I promise I had nothing to do with any of this and was ready to talk to you this afternoon. And I'm not going to say anything that's not true and I'll tell you everything I can. But…"

Tim and Dexter returned with some chairs. Willis nodded to Maggie that he understood, but he still looked unhappy.

The men settled themselves. Dexter and Willis pulled out notebooks.

"You've read the files I sent you?" Tim asked Dexter.

"Yes. Verney, Walker and Greenaway."

"Good. So I'll let Maggie begin."

So Maggie began with her concerns about the death of Charlotte Verney. She felt like Homer being asked to recite the *Odyssey*. Again. Bring on the rosy-fingered dawn. She knew what she was going to say by heart.

"But I knew Inspector Willis considered the cases closed. And there was certainly no hard evidence against Marsh. So I let it drop until one day, I saw Marsh again. At Beaumatin. He was going to speak at some seminars at Rochford Manor. And help shepherd the attendees through some garden tours. At Beaumatin as well as Rochford Manor.

"And it occurred to me. That it was snowdrop season and that if he did have the Beaumatin's Blondes that Greenaway was assumed to have taken and given to Walker, they might be in bloom. And identifiable. There are only twenty-four of the plants and we know where eighteen are. So if he had the other six…

"The problem was, Marsh is paranoid. About poachers. Perhaps with cause as he is one himself. So he grows his plants in a secret garden. No one knows where it is. And it is rumoured to be guarded by…"

Tim held up his hand.

"Let me indicate for the record that Lady Raynham and I had lunch and she told me about her concerns and I told her I would try to help her find out the location of the garden. And also that Lennox Archibald-Atherton, who does some consulting with my department, might be able to assist her.

"We identified Marsh's garden through a title search. It was in the name of Marsh's grandmother, one Gertrude Jenkins. Marsh had inherited the land on her death but had never had the title transferred. Please continue, Maggie."

Maggie frowned. "I hope I am getting the sequence of events right. I think next… There is an annual event. A snowdrop ball. Well, you know about that," she said to Dexter. He nodded.

"This year it was held in London. And Marsh was supposed to come. As an escort to Lady Sarah Archibald-Atherton, who is an RHS Vice President. And Lennox's aunt. At the last minute Marsh claimed he couldn't make it because of an emergency. I thought it might be because he saw it as a perfect opportunity to steal some snowdrops. I was worried about… Anyhow, one couple who was there, the Epsleys, did have their garden robbed. Their entire collection was stolen.

"So we knew where Marsh's garden was and I wanted to see if indeed the Beaumatin's Blondes were there. And now the Epsleys' snowdrops as well. Marsh was speaking at a seminar on snowdrops being held at Rochford Manor so it seemed safe to… explore.

"I know what I did would probably be considered trespassing. Is it trespassing if one is trying to find stolen property? Anyway, I did find the Beaumatin's Blondes in Marsh's garden. And the Chloe Symeons. But Marsh surprised us…"

"Us?" said Willis.

"Archibald-Atherton accompanied Lady Raynham," conceded Tim. "As a witness."

"So I went back the following week. This time I was specifically looking for the Epsleys' snowdrops. I found a grouping that had most of the cultivars the Epsleys said were missing, but I also found… well some animal had been digging where the snowdrops had been planted. And there were some… bones."

"Was Archibald-Atherton with you?" demanded Willis,

"No."

"All right."

"But we met shortly after. And I showed him the bones—I took some samples. I thought he might have a better idea if they were human…"

"And why would you have a better idea," Willis asked Lennox.

"That's classified," said Tim.

Willis scowled.

"Anyway, we went back and Archi… is it all right if I just say Lennox? Lennox went to see while I… waited for him. He saw some more bones plus… well shouldn't Lennox tell you this?"

Tim nodded. Lennox continued.

"I found where the snowdrops had been dug up and some bone fragments. And I also saw two concave depressions in the earth that in my experience were the size and shape to indicate a grave."

"And you did what?" demanded Willis.

Maggie answered.

"The problem was… well we were, er, trespassing. And I didn't want to do anything to alert Marsh. For fear he'd destroy the evidence. The snowdrops as well as the bones."

"We were considering our options. Then, um, was it yesterday? Really only yesterday?"

"Yes," said Willis.

"I was in one of the gardens at Beaumatin taking photographs. Of some snowdrops. It was the area where our most rare and valuable plants are kept. It's surrounded by a stone wall and can only be entered through a door that is normally kept locked.

"Although it's been pointed out to me that it you look at Beaumatin using a Google satellite image you can clearly see the rectangle. And the door isn't hidden, even if it isn't blatantly obvious.

"And Marsh had been in the gardens several times quite recently. He could have easily noticed the door. And assumed there would be a secure area where the special snowdrops were kept. And also looked at Google.

"Anyway I was in the walled garden. I'd been taking pictures of the snowdrops and Marsh came in. I confronted him and he had a jar—I think Lord Raynham gave it to you?" Maggie asked Willis, who nodded.

"Marsh said it contained botrytis. Botrytis is a fungus that's lethal to snowdrops and once it's in the soil there's nothing you can do. Anyhow he threatened to spill the contents of the jar in the garden unless I showed him where a particular snowdrop was. I tried to stall him…"

"What snowdrop was that?" asked Dexter.

"Um… the Ainswick Orange. Which had been stolen from Rochford Manor last year, as I believe you know. For some reason Marsh seemed to be convinced it was at Beaumatin."

Maggie hurried on. "As I said, I was trying to stall him when Thomas came out to look for me. And Marsh pulled out a knife and just attacked him. With no warning. Oh, and he threw the jar at a wall. I guess he hoped it would break. But I managed to catch it. If I'd known he was going to attack Thomas, I really would have been between Scylla and Charybdis."

"Between what?" asked Willis.

"A rock and a hard place," said Lennox.

"And then Lennox came in and Marsh attacked him too. He… it was much worse than with Thomas, whom Marsh only stabbed in the arm. And I was afraid Marsh would do more damage so I… I whacked him with my camera."

"You broke his nose," said Willis.

"Did I? Good."

Willis shook his head while Dexter tried not to smile.

"He dropped his knife. I tried to pick it up but he… stomped on my arm. With his boot. More than once." Maggie sounded indignant. She indicated her cast.

The men tried not to wince.

"Then Mr Pilchard…" Maggie looked at Tim.

"Mr Pilchard works for my department and was assisting Mr Archibald-Atherton, as we do consider someone who commits multiple murders to be a security issue. All you need to know is that Mr Pilchard subdued Marsh and kept him under guard until you arrived. I believe he showed you his identification?" Tim asked Willis.

"Yes," said Willis grudgingly.

"Very well."

"Let's go back a moment," said Willis.

"What were you doing at Beaumatin?" he asked Lennox.

"I had been following Marsh. I knew Lady Raynham had been concerned about whether he might try to poach some plants from Beaumatin. If he did, and were caught, we thought it might open the possibility for further investigation."

"So it was just luck that you and Pilchard turned up when you did."

"Not soon enough to prevent him from attacking Lord Raynham, unfortunately."

"Then why does Marsh say you offered him £10,000 to steal the Ainswick Orange from that garden at Beaumatin? That you showed him where the door was. And gave him a cheque for £5,000, with the rest to be paid on delivery."

"Indeed? He said that? He must be quite mad. Or desperate." Lennox dripped disdain.

Maggie thought Lennox must be channelling Thomas. Unless disdain was something they taught you at Eton.

"He said it was for your aunt."

"For Aunt Sarah? She doesn't even like snowdrops particularly. Auriculas are her speciality. She even has one of those Victorian theatre display thingies. You can ask anyone. Although I'd be careful if I did. She'd be sure to find out and she can be a real dragon, Aunt Sarah."

Willis was looking unhappy again. Probably imagining a future directing traffic in Stroud if he antagonised Lady Sarah Archibald-Atherton.

"Have your questions been answered, Detectives?" Tim asked.

"For now," said Dexter. "I am sure there will be additional issues. And of course we will need to search that garden of Marsh's. And his house."

The men had risen to go when the door opened and Thomas walked in. He stopped short and looked at the group.

"Well, I would not have been surprised to see Inspector Willis. Although I would have expected my son to have been present as well." He looked at Maggie and his eyes were cold.

"But Detective Chief Inspector Dexter, you're here too. Has Scotland Yard been called in over an attempt to poach some snowdrops that got... a bit out of hand?

"And you also, young Lennox."

Thomas nudged the wheel chair with his toe and it moved forward a bit.

"Shouldn't you really be in bed? I know it took Lady Raynham weeks to recover when she was stabbed last year.

"And finally... Tim, isn't it? If that is your name. Did you really come all the way to Cheltenham over some small white flowers or did the plans for the deployment of our troops in Afghanistan turn up in Marsh's Highgrove bag?"

Maggie decided she had been wrong when she thought Lennox was channelling Thomas. Thomas' mastery of the disdainful tone was Olympic gold medal quality. Lennox was still trying to qualify for the finals.

She also realised how furious Thomas was and wished aliens would suddenly appear and decide to beam her up into their space ship. She was sure they would find the pins in her arm interesting to study.

"Or is a mere husband not permitted to know what is going on. Even when it centres on his wife?"

He turned to Maggie. "Mrs Cook remembered how much you dislike hospital food. She drove me over with some soup."

He set a bag down on her hospital tray.

"I'm afraid you'll need to ask one of the staff for help. The thermos needs two hands to open it. Or perhaps Archibald-Atherton here can assist you. I'm sure there's enough to share."

Tim intervened. "Lord Raynham, I am sure you would like to be informed about what has been going on. If you'd come with us," he indicated Dexter and Willis, "We will tell you. And give our patients the opportunity to rest."

The men left. Thomas did not look at Maggie again.

Lennox eyed the bag.

"Soup?"

Maggie gave a strangled laugh.

"No. It's all yours. Just return the thermos, please, to avoid…"

She stopped abruptly.

"Maggie?"

Lennox got out of his chair.

"Are you all right?"

He saw her tears.

"I'm sorry," she sniffed. "It's just… my arm. It's extremely sore."

"As is his lordship," Lennox added.

"Yes. That too."

"That was an impressive performance. I don't think I've ever seen Tim be conciliatory before. Usually he fights ice with, well, more ice."

"Thomas says it's the result of eight hundred years of breeding. And a lot of practice."

"Hmm. All very well. Except when it's directed at you, I expect."

They looked at each other.

"I understand you should be sprung from here tomorrow?"

"I think that's the plan."

"You'll be all right?"

Maggie nodded.

"It's a pity Tim has probably had The Fish remove the caravan by now. Otherwise I would have wanted to put up a plaque."

He was glad to see that got a smile from Maggie.

He kissed her, one eye on the door.

"Take care, Moppet. And keep the phone. Crispin is as close as *1."

He put the bag of soup on the seat of the wheelchair and then left, pushing it in front of him.

Chapter 29

Mrs Cook came to fetch Maggie the next morning. She had not seen or heard from Thomas since he had left with Tim the day before. She assumed that meant he was still furious.

Maggie was given a bottle of medication for pain, told to keep her arm elevated and to return in a week for a check-up. She stopped by Lennox's room to say goodbye but his bed was empty. The thermos was sitting on a bedside table, with a red rose lying beside it. Perhaps a black helicopter had come after all.

"His lordship's arm is bothering him," said Mrs Cook, explaining Thomas' absence.

"That was a terrible thing that Marsh did. And I wasn't there. I'd never forgive myself if…"

She did not need to finish her sentence.

Maggie did not see Thomas when she arrived back at Beaumatin. She had thought he would at least be there to greet her.

"Fine. Just fine," she thought.

As usual after a hospital stay, the first thing Maggie wanted to do was wash. She went to her room, wiggled out of her clothes, put a plastic bag over her cast, and attempted to shower. She found showering with one hand difficult and washing her hair almost impossible.

How did one open a bottle of shampoo with one hand? She dropped the bottle twice before she got the cap off. The plastic bag came off her cast and it got wet. Her facial wash was also impossible to open. She gave up and used a cake of soap.

She came out of the bathroom and went into her clothes closet. What pants could she get into with one hand to fasten them, assuming she could even pull them up? And did she have any tops that would fit over the cast? Possibly one of her fisherman's sweaters. She certainly could not manage a bra.

Maggie pulled on some briefs. Then laid a pair of jeans on the bed. She used a knee to hold them while she unfastened a snap and undid the zipper. She sat on the bed and dangled the jeans with one hand. She leaned over and put one leg in, pulled up the pants, then pushed them back down when she realised she couldn't get the other leg in. With both legs in she realised she couldn't stand while she pulled the pants up as she was standing on the fabric. It took her five minutes to get the jeans on and her arm was throbbing.

The sweater was easier, although the cast made the sleeve very tight and pushing it through the sleeve just made her arm hurt more.

She slipped on some loafers. At least that was easy.

Then she realised she needed to fix her hair. She ruffled the curls into some semblance of order but after several failed attempts realised there was no way she could put in a hair clip. She needed both hands.

"Pig-headed," came a voice.

Maggie whirled around.

Thomas was sitting in one of the chairs. The bedroom was dim and she hadn't noticed him. She wondered how long he had been watching her.

"I hope you've been entertained." Her voice sounded strained.

"A video would go viral on YouTube overnight, I'm sure. Pity I didn't have a camera."

"Yes. Well."

"You could have asked for help, you know."

"I didn't realise there was anyone I could ask."

There was silence. Then Thomas got up and walked over to her. He removed the hair clip from her hand and turned her around. He gently pulled her curls back and caught them in the clip. Maggie noticed he wasn't wearing his sling.

"Like I said. Pig-headed," he murmured in her ear, standing close behind her.

Maggie smelled his wonderful citrusy-spicy aftershave and felt tears start.

"You are not as lesser woman, Maggie Eliot," she told herself fiercely. "Only a lesser woman would cry because her husband is being carelessly kind."

He wrapped his arms around her and held her tightly against him.

"I understand from the, um, authorities that you've been busy. Maggie Eliot, Ace Detective, in fact."

He turned her around and looked down at her. He rubbed a tear away with a fingertip.

"Paul Dexter has promised to keep me informed. As I could not be sure at this point that you would."

He took out the hair clip he had just put in. Then he moved Maggie back and gently pushed her down onto the bed.

"And in the meantime, I am going to remove these jeans that I so much appreciated your struggles to get into. And later I intend to enjoy watching you try to put them back on again."

Chapter 30

After lunch, which was soup, eaten inelegantly by Maggie with her left hand, Dexter appeared and he and Thomas drove off. Thomas did not tell her why and she was too proud to ask. Perhaps they were going to a pub for a drink and some guy talk. Even though Maggie had never known Thomas to go to a pub. Well, there was a first time for everything, she supposed.

Her emails were stacked up and Maggie spent the afternoon dealing with the backlog. With one hand, it took time. And she used her mouse with her right hand as well. She would be more appreciative of her two-handedness in the future and not take it for granted, she decided.

Thomas was out with Dexter all afternoon. When he came back, he looked shaken.

"Dexter took me to Marsh's garden to do some snowdrop identification. The Beaumatin's Blondes are there…"

"Well, I told you that."

"Yes, you did. And the Chloe Symeons. And the Epsleys' collection. Dexter had a list. And the other cultivars that went missing from Rochford Manor. And I saw Marsh's Gnat. And the other Marsh Galanthus. The SOCOs made me put on one of those blue overall suit thingies. So I didn't contaminate anything. A unique experience.

"And Archibald-Atherton was right. They found two other graves. They had cadaver dogs there that were going through the woods. I gather there are quite a few acres. But they hadn't found any more than the two, plus the bones that were under the Epsleys' snowdrops. I'm afraid the Epsleys will not be seeing their collection again. But I did make a plea for the Blondes. Dexter couldn't promise, but he was hopeful."

"Any other news?"

"I don't know. I gather at some point we'll get a visit. Willis was particularly unhappy. He went out of his way to tell me he should have paid more attention to you. For once I couldn't object."

"Yes. Are we going to talk about that?"

"Yes, Papillon. But not right now. I'm a bit... shattered."

Thomas was rubbing his arm where he'd been stabbed. Maggie noticed.

"Can I get you some Laphroaig?"

"Do you think you could open the bottle with one hand? That's all right. I'll get some. But thank you."

"I'd offer to kiss your arm and make it all better, like adults did to me when I was five, but I suspect some Laphroaig will be more effective."

Thomas pulled her close and buried his face in her curls.

"I suspect you're right."

Chapter 31

The next morning, Thomas came into Maggie's study and announced, "Dexter called. He and Willis and I imagine young Sergeant Patrick will be coming by this afternoon."

"Do you know why? Is it something specific or are they just letting us know what's happening?"

"I'm not sure."

"Well at least we don't need to worry about anyone's being arrested."

"I sincerely hope not," agreed Thomas.

At three o'clock, Dexter and Willis arrived, without Sergeant Patrick, who was overseeing the search of Marsh's house.

They met in the drawing room, at Maggie's request. The detectives inquired after Maggie's arm.

"It's all right, thank you," she insisted.

The policemen exchanged "Yeah, right," glances.

Mrs Cook appeared with coffee, tea and some homemade teacakes. Dexter immediately looked more cheerful.

Thomas served, and then waited.

Dexter led off.

"We have finished searching Marsh's garden and believe there are only the three graves. A forensic anthropologist and her team are recovering the skeletons. She believes there are two women and one man. One of the women died around a decade ago, the man around two years ago and the second woman as recently as last year. The bones you found are from the oldest burial."

"Do you know how they died?" Maggie asked.

"No. It is much too early to tell. Or even to attempt an identification except for gender."

"Has Marsh said anything? About the bodies?" asked Thomas.

"No. He's not talking, except to urge us to be careful of his snowdrops."

Maggie and Thomas exchanged glances. They could relate to that.

"And the snowdrops? The ones that were taken from Rochford Manor?"

"He says he accepted them from Greenaway in good faith."

Maggie sighed. She had anticipated Marsh might use the "Greenaway defence."

"The other thing is, we're searching Marsh's house. But it's slow going. Marsh is a hoarder."

"Really? Newspapers to the ceiling with narrow canyon pathways?" Maggie asked.

"No. No newspapers. Thankfully. Marsh is not a reader, it seems. But it looks like he kept everything that ever came into the house. Except what he used for compost. String. Rubber bands. Paper clips. Clothing. We found a milk container with a sell-by date of 2003. In a box with dozens of other milk containers that had been carefully washed out, flattened and stacked. Another box had the plastic wrappers from loaves of bread. Another had cans that were washed and flattened. The ends were stacked according to size. He's apparently a big eater of beans on toast," Dexter said.

"It's seriously creepy," added Willis. "There are five bedrooms. Three are full of Marsh's hoardings, one is half full except for a cot where he must sleep, and one bedroom that was obviously his mother's. That's untouched. He's kept it as a shrine. And it's clean. Dusted. Vacuumed.

"But it's going to take some time to go through everything and see if there's anything in there that connects Marsh to the earlier deaths. And the bodies from the garden, assuming we can get identification and causes of death."

"There is one thing," he continued.

"The coroner thinks the knife Marsh used to attack Archibald-Atherton and you," he turned to Thomas, "could be a match to the one used to kill Linda Walker."

"Really?" said Maggie.

Willis nodded.

Well that was something, Maggie thought.

"And did you find out anything about Marsh's financial situation?"

"His mother left him the house and around £50,000. He has a modest account balance. Around £5,000. Pays his bills on time. Claims annual income of around £20,000, more or less."

Maggie tried to estimate if that figure matched with the sums she'd seen him collect from his galanthophile clients. She realised she had no idea. Well, she'd leave that to the experts.

"Have you heard anything from your Whitehall mates?" Willis asked Maggie.

"No. No, but I hadn't expected to," said Maggie.

Willis looked sceptical and Maggie was aware that Thomas was also watching her.

"No. Truly," she repeated.

"If you say so," Willis finally said.

The detectives stood. Maggie and Thomas stood.

"Thank you for keeping us informed. Obviously, anything else we can do to help…"

Dexter nodded.

Let me show you out," said Thomas.

Maggie waited. After the intensity of the past weeks, she was feeling a bit let down. Even more so now with the investigation grinding on but with no dramatic results. Well she supposed the bodies in Marsh's garden were dramatic. And the news about the knife. But still…

What had she been expecting? She was no longer sure she knew. Her cast was irksome, her arm hurt and she was dreading the conversation—or confrontation--she knew was coming with Thomas.

The man himself returned. He studied Maggie, whose hair clip had become dislodged and whose curls were looking even more than usually unruly.

"So?" she asked quietly.

"So."

"Thomas… I'm sorry."

"Sorry?"

Maggie was silent.

"What I want to know is, how much of the past weeks has been real and how much was just a… a smoke screen you created to keep me from finding out what was really going on."

"There was no smoke screen."

"No? I don't believe you."

"Look. You know I thought Marsh was somehow involved with the deaths of Walker and Greenaway. And Charlotte. And that he had the Beaumatin's Blondes. And the other Rochford Manor snowdrops that went missing. In his secret garden.

"And it was snowdrop season. So they could be identified. If it were possible to find it. Marsh's garden. But when I'd try to talk to you about it, you'd get angry and tell me I was being a crackpot. And pig-headed. And obsessed. Do you know how frustrating that is? When no one will listen to you? I guess you don't."

"No, you're right. I don't. The only person who doesn't listen to me is you."

"Yes. The pig-headed crackpot. Well, maybe I am pig-headed. But I'm not a crackpot. So…"

"So you went to Tim. And Archibald-Atherton."

"Yes. To Tim. Who did listen. And offered Archibald-Atherton's help. And we found the garden. And the Beaumatin's Blondes and the other snowdrops. But I was only there twice. Once with Archibald-Atherton and once with Anne."

"And the rest of it?"

"The rest?"

"Your interest in the gardens here? The RHS Show? The seminars? The photography? Were you even at the seminars?"

"Yes. Yes, of course I was. What do you think? And my helping at the RHS Show? And my wanting to take pictures? And my interest in the gardens here? That was real. That had nothing at all to do with Marsh." Maggie was indignant.

"Humpf."

"Humpf yourself, Thomas Raynham. No, I know," she held up her hand. "But I can't call you Raynham. The way Beatrix calls Cedric, Ainswick. So Thomas, then."

"I don't know what to believe. Or whether I can trust you."

"Of course you can trust me. But you also need to listen to me. And when we have a disagreement, you can't just think you can resolve things by telling me what to do. Or dismiss me by calling me names. I'm not going to go along with something I don't agree with simply because you say so."

"What is it that you say? If only."

"Thomas!"

Thomas paced.

"Thomas, I'm sorry I, um, deceived you. But I didn't feel like I had a choice. And even if I don't care that much about Walker, or Greenaway, I do care about Emily. If I could make things even a little better for her…"

Thomas knew Emily had found her mother. And that Maggie had found Emily with Charlotte. It was a scene he avoided thinking about.

He sighed.

"Papillon, you've lost your hair clip."

He bent over, picked it up, and began to gently pull her hair back.

"I should have known that any woman who had such unruly hair would be… unmanageable."

Maggie was about to say she certainly was not about to be managed, but thought better of it.

"Yes. I'd have thought it should have been obvious."

Thomas' mouth twitched.

SUSAN ALEXANDER

Chapter 32

The snowdrop season was drawing to a close. However, unlike the previous year, which had had an early spring, this year winter lingered, so the later-blooming snowdrops held on and there were no signs of bulbs or fruit trees beginning to flower.

Malcolm Fortescue-Smythe had heard about Maggie's unspecified accident and paid a visit to Beaumatin. Her book continued to be on the bestseller list, although with time it was moving lower in the rankings. Maggie gave it two more weeks before she could return to literary obscurity.

However, in the meantime, with time on her hands even though she lacked a hand, or perhaps because she lacked a hand, she had had an idea for a book for Malcolm.

Maggie explained over coffee.

"Your interest in snowdrops got me thinking. I mean, it is in fact ridiculous to pay hundreds of pounds for a bulb that produces small white flowers with only miniscule differences from similar small white flowers. One has to ask, well, questions of value. Fundamental value. And why we value what we do. The way we do. I mean, why is a VW considered to be better than a Ford? Or why are Versace jeans more expensive than Levis? Why, if you stick an alligator or polo player on a shirt, is it better than one without one? Better in the sense that people will pay more to buy it.

"And if you look at different cultures, you find different things are valued. Or I believe you do. Although certainly the Chinese are buying their fair share of Birkin bags these days. Anyhow, given my credentials in cultural relativism, and the Zeitgeist in general, I thought it could be interesting. How we value stuff. And what it says about us. What do you think?"

"I think it might be interesting. Could you do a one- or two-pager and I'll show it to some people? It won't do for the Developing World series, but it would certainly fit in with Great Issues. Like your current opus."

"Which is still selling well to my eternal delight and which has even had carry over effects to some of the other Great Issues volumes."

"You must be pleased."

"People who would never deign to notice a mere academic publisher at the Arts Club are buying me drinks. While pitching me their ideas for their own books, needless to say."

Maggie laughed.

Thomas came in, still in his riding clothes.

"Malcolm."

"Thomas."

Hands were shaken.

"I assume you are plotting with our best-selling author about how to continue her run."

"Indeed. And she has even come up with an interesting idea."

"Oh? You must tell me about it," he said to Maggie.

"And Malcolm. Can I convince you to stay for supper? Spend the night?"

"Um. That's very kind. Include a tour of the gardens and your famous snowdrops and I may allow myself to be persuaded."

"It would be a pleasure. Although we are past the height of the season, there are still some about. Just let me change."

Maggie reflected that Thomas seemed to be in an unusually good mood. Had one of the sheep produced a Golden Fleece, she wondered.

Thomas went off.

"You're warned. Although the Bordeaux will be excellent, there is a good chance that that supper will be shepherd's pie. Or chicken pie. Or beef and kidney pie. Or…"

Malcolm held up his hand.

"That would be wonderful. I love a good pie."

Oh dear. I should tell Mrs Cook, thought Maggie.

In fact, Mrs Cook produced a steak and kidney pudding, to the men's delight. Afterwards Thomas and Malcolm played billiards, with Maggie an attentive but neutral audience.

Malcolm was still bemused by the snowdrops.

"Not that they're not pretty. But I'm certainly not sure I can tell the difference between your £4 nivalis and your £40 um is it Diggory? There are the ones with bits of yellow, of course, but they're yellow. You can see that right away. And the ones with green on the petals outside. You can see that too.

"I liked your hellebores, weren't they? Different shapes. Different colours. And that was nice the way you had the flowers floating in that bowl at dinner. But unless I'm mistaken, no one has paid £700 for one of them, right?"

He turned to Maggie while Thomas took his turn.

"So perhaps you're on to something with that idea for your new book. When do you think you could have it done? May? June?"

Maggie gave a startled laugh.

"Malcolm. I researched the last book for six months and it took another four to write. And your Great Issues version was also based on that work. And that built on research I'd already done. I haven't even begun to think about the work this book will require. The research…"

Thomas paused.

"Ah. You mentioned a new book…"

"Yes. About why, um, a new hellebore sells for £30 pounds while a snowdrop can sell for £300. It's not about quality, like why a Bordeaux sells for more than plonk. And, in many cases, with snowdrops, the differences are miniscule. As you know. Anyhow, for me it brings up the whole issue of why we value things the way we do. And there are cultural differences. Which would tie into my previous work.

"However, I will need to do some thinking. And searches through the literature…"

"As long as you don't have to search in Tierra del Fuego. Or Micronesia," Thomas said.

"But I already booked my tickets to Dushanbe…" Maggie began.

"Dushanbe?"

"It's the capital of Tajikistan," Maggie explained.

Thomas realised Maggie was joking. Or he hoped she was. He was happy for her to have a new project. As long as she could do it at Beaumatin.

Maggie noticed what had begun as a nearly full bottle of Laphroaig was now nearly empty. Hmm. She had better retreat while the men were still able to stand upright. With her broken arm she would hardly be able to help one up the stairs. And certainly not two. She just hoped they didn't start singing.

She excused herself.

Maggie was just dozing off when her door opened. Thomas peeked in.

"Maggie?"

"Yes?"

"You're in bed."

He came in and closed the door.

"Yes. I was tired."

He was wearing his blue silk paisley robe. He slipped it off and slid in beside her.

"Well. I hope you're not too tired."

Susan Alexander

Chapter 33

Dexter and Willis came by unexpectedly the next afternoon. Malcolm had departed for London and Thomas was out with Ned and the sheep. Maggie invited them to meet in her study.

"Is this where you write your best sellers?" Dexter asked.

"Hmm. This is more where I answer emails and read the latest academic journals."

Mrs Cook brought in coffee and tea and helped serve.

When she had left, Dexter began, "We have some news. And a request."

The men shared a glance and Maggie wondered what was going on.

"First. We finished the search of Marsh's house. And found... well we found a bottle of barbiturates. In his mother's bathroom. Which he had also kept as she left it. The pills were the same sort that Charlotte Verney took."

"Or was given."

"Or was given," the detective conceded.

"They were a bit beyond their sell-by date but the pathologist thinks they would still have been effective enough. We also found a coil of rope in Marsh's rope box— he had a box of different sorts of rope all neatly rolled up in varying lengths along with the cans and the milk containers and, well, you get the idea.

"The rope is believed to match the one that was used in Charlotte's hanging. We were lucky that we still had a sample. It might have been thrown away once her death had been ruled a suicide. Forensics is verifying that it's the same."

"We also found Marsh's money box. Under his mother's bed. It had close to £100,000 in it. All sorted into tens and twenties and fifties and hundreds and each type of note bound in packs with rubber bands."

"Oh."

Maggie thought.

"Do you think he can invoke insanity as a defence?"

"If I were his solicitor, I certainly would," said Willis.

"And the bodies in the garden?"

"We're checking missing person reports. And eventually dental records."

"Oh."

Maggie expected the men would now leave. But they didn't. The detectives glanced at each other again.

"There is one more thing," Willis said.

"Yes?"

"Marsh has refused to say anything. About anything. To anyone. Except to say he got your, er, Blondes from Greenaway. And to accuse Archibald-Atherton of being behind his presence in your garden."

"I suppose that makes sense. Not saying anything."

"But he's finally said he'll talk. On one condition."

Maggie wondered briefly if the condition involved the Ainswick Orange.

"Yes?"

"He said he'll talk. But only to you."

"Me?"

Willis nodded.

"Why me?"

"No idea. It's my opinion he's a complete nutter and trying to figure out the reasons crazy people do what they do is a waste of time, in my experience. I'll leave that to the psychiatrists. But DCI Dexter and I, we thought we'd ask. If you'd be willing…"

"Of course. Anything I can do to help."

"But he insists it be just the two of you. Alone."

"Alone? Not with one or both of you?"

"Alone." Dexter confirmed.

"Naturally we'll have some sort of camera. So we can watch. And listen. We wouldn't put you at risk. But maybe he'd tell you who those bodies in the garden are," said Willis.

"And about Charlotte."

"And about Charlotte," agreed Willis.

"All right."

"Um. Don't you want to ask Lord Raynham?" Dexter inquired.

"Ask him? For permission?" Maggie said in a tone that made the detectives look at each other nervously.

"Ask my permission for what?" came a voice from the doorway.

Thomas had returned. Maggie's stomach went wobbly when she saw him and she thought he looked particularly fine in his riding clothes that day.

"Er..." Dexter began.

"Marsh wants to talk to me. Apparently he is refusing to talk to everyone else," Maggie explained.

Thomas looked less than thrilled.

"Well, it will be in an interview room, right? With one of you. A PC..."

"No. I'm afraid he insists they talk alone," Dexter explained.

"Alone?"

"Just the two of them."

"But why?"

The detectives shrugged.

"He's a nutter. Who knows why," said Willis.

Now Thomas was scowling.

"I don't know..."

"Thomas?"

It was Maggie.

"Yes?"

"I don't expect it will be pleasant. But I'm sure I'll be fine. And if it means getting some answers…"

"We'll have the room under surveillance," Dexter told the increasingly frosty baron.

"Humpf."

"And if he's just playing games, I'll simply get up and leave."

Maggie watched Thomas and knew without him having to say a word what he was thinking.

Pig-headed.

But being fairly certain Maggie would go ahead and do it anyway, Thomas said, "Very well. But I am coming with you. You will need to wait while I change."

He walked out.

Maggie looked relieved.

"Well, that went well."

She paused.

"I'd also like to take a moment and wash. If that's all right."

Thomas and Maggie followed Willis and Dexter in Maggie's Land Rover. It was a quiet ride. Maggie was nervous and Thomas, she suspected, was fuming.

When they were led to the interview room where Marsh was waiting, Maggie was surprised to see Crispin.

Lennox. He held himself stiffly. Maggie assumed he was still recovering from the knife wound. She could relate to that.

Thomas scowled.

"Archibald-Atherton."

"Raynham."

"To what do we owe the pleasure?"

"Follow-up."

Maggie decided to intervene before it got to pistols at ten paces.

"So what happens next?" she asked the detectives.

"Marsh is in there." Willis indicated a metal door.

"We have a camera. Sound. The door will be locked from inside, but not out, and we'll hear and see everything. If you feel uncomfortable or that Marsh is just messing with you, let us know and we'll come right in."

Maggie nodded. She was not quite clear about how she would let them know, but assumed when the time came, she would figure something out.

"All right, then. Let's, um, do this."

Willis opened the door and went in, followed by Maggie.

"You said if Lady Raynham came, you'd speak with her. Answer her questions. So here she is."

"I said alone."

"If you're willing to talk to her, I'll leave."

"Leave."

Maggie sat down across from Marsh at a small metal table that was bolted to the floor. Their chairs were also fixed securely.

"Well, Marsh?"

Maggie was disturbed by Marsh's appearance. His hair was no longer dull, but dark with grease and stuck together in messy locks. His face seemed to have drooped—he looked ten years older—and his eyes were, well, strange. Not just that they were still blackened. They would dart around the room and then seem to lose focus. His left ear was bandaged. And he exuded a strange, musty smell. Like a cellar that suffered from damp.

Marsh stared at Maggie. Then his eyes fell to her cast and he tried to hide a smirk.

"Marsh, you said you wanted to talk."

"Yes. I want to talk."

"All right."

Maggie realised she was sounding hostile. Probably not a good idea if she wanted Marsh to answer her questions.

"You can catch more flies with honey than you can with vinegar," was one of her mother's favourite sayings.

"How are my snowdrops?" he finally asked.

"We asked the police to be as careful as possible. I think they are doing their best not to cause any unnecessary damage."

Marsh looked like he wanted to believe her.

"So what do you want to know?"

Maggie became aware that neither Dexter nor Willis had told her what was most important for her to find out. So she decided to ask what was most important to her.

"About Charlotte. Verney. She was found hanging from a tree. She'd taken, or been given, barbiturates. But I can't believe she killed herself. Did she? Or was she murdered?"

"That was Greenaway. And that Walker woman. Greenaway had convinced Verney that he cared about her. To make it easier to take the Rochford Manor snowdrops. Verney was too busy mooning over him to notice what was really happening. Stupid bitch.

"But Walker was worried that Greenaway might actually be starting to care for Verney. She got jealous. And then Verney saw Greenaway pocketing some snowdrops. He made up an excuse, but she was getting suspicious. And began to watch Greenaway more closely.

"He was afraid she would say something to the Ainswicks. So she had to go. Walker and Greenaway managed it between them."

"But you helped too."

"Only with some pills. And some rope."

Maggie felt relief mixed with sadness. Poor Charlotte. But at least Emily could be told her mother had not abandoned her in such a cruel, dreadful way. It wouldn't bring Charlotte back, but she hoped it would help.

Maggie moved on.

"And Walker?"

"Another stupid bitch. I never knew what Greenaway saw in her. She helped herself to some of the snowdrops Greenaway had taken for me. Offered them for sale online. The connection was too direct. No one would wonder if I were selling an Esther Merton or Phil Cornish, even if some were found to have gone missing from Rochford Manor. But Linda's Snowdrop Gardens?" Marsh said the name contemptuously.

"And thinking if she called Chloe Symeon Cleopatra that no one would notice they were the same? She had to go. I knew Greenaway was too weak to do anything, so I took care of it myself."

"So you killed Walker. With the same knife you used to stab Archibald-Atherton. And Lord Raynham."

Marsh nodded.

"But the police thought that Greenaway had killed Walker," Maggie went on.

"Well, the boyfriend is always at the top of the suspect list, isn't he? Greenaway had no alibi. And he and Walker had had some fights about Verney that people had witnessed. I wasn't even a blip on the fuzz's radar. Until you mentioned me."

Marsh glared at her.

"But then Greenaway panicked and was killed before he could rat me out. Too bad for him, Lucky for me."

"He was killed because you helped tip the ladder he was on. And sent him crashing through the glass."

"But you were the only one who noticed that. And with Greenaway's death, the police considered the cases closed."

Marsh smirked.

"Gardeners. So badly paid. Doing such backbreaking labour. Considered menials by their employers. Who take all the credit for their hard work. It's so easy to play on their resentment. And greed."

Maggie noticed the plural.

"Had you done the same before? With other gardeners?"

"Just one."

Maggie waited.

"He was working in a garden in Malvern that was known for its snowdrop collection. When you separate a clump, who's to know if a bulb or two goes missing. If he saw something unusual, he would tell me and not the owner, who would take the credit anyway. He was happy to get a percentage of what I sold. Until he got greedy. And wanted more. He threatened me. So I moved on. To Greenaway."

"And this gardener from Malvern. He didn't do anything? When you moved on?"

Marsh's face became closed. Secretive. He rubbed his hands together.

"He liked snowdrops. So I put him…"

Maggie made an intuitive leap.

"You killed him and buried him in your secret garden. Did you stab him too?"

"Yes. How did you…"

"The police found three bodies. Or skeletons. Who are the other two?"

Marsh gave Maggie what her mother would call a dirty look. She was glad Willis and Dexter and Crispin were watching and listening.

"One was just another stupid bitch. Why are you women so stupid? Is it your hormones? This woman was a collector. From Oxfordshire. She decided to…

"She began following me. To try to discover my garden. But I noticed. She drove a white BMW and she'd been too obvious. So I decided to lead her there. To my garden. I left the gate ajar and waited. She came back. I found her digging up a Moses Basket. And made sure she'd never poach a snowdrop again. Or tell anyone else where my garden was."

Maggie hoped Marsh had given enough detail for Dexter and Willis to identify the woman.

"And the third?"

Marsh had become withdrawn.

"The third, Marsh?"

"That was my mother."

"Your mother?"

"Yes. The only woman I ever knew who wasn't a stupid bitch."

Marsh closed his eyes. Then opened them.

"She also loved snowdrops. I wanted to keep her close."

Maggie wanted to ask how Mrs Marsh had died, but something prevented her. It was all getting very Norman Bates.

"Very well. Thank you."

Marsh roused himself.

"I've answered your questions?"

He said it with a sneer.

"Yes. Most of them."

"Good. Now I have one for you."

"All right."

"How does it feel to be another stupid bitch who's about to die?"

And without warning, Marsh leapt at her. He had some pointy object in his hand. Maggie instinctively threw up her arm to defend herself but Marsh's momentum carried him forward. The object lodged in her cast.

Marsh cursed. He grabbed Maggie's hand and yanked her towards him to recover his shiv.

Maggie screamed.

Chapter 34

The men had been watching and listening to what amounted to Marsh's confession.

"But we can't use this in court," Dexter warned Willis.

"Yes. But with this information we can get forensics. Identify the victims. Question him again. I can't imagine he'll shut up once he's told Mag... er, Lady Raynham all this."

Marsh had gotten to his mother.

"I don't like this," Crispin said suddenly.

He moved towards the door.

"Hey. Wait. Don't you..." Willis protested.

Crispin burst into the interview room just as Marsh drove his shiv into Maggie's cast.

"Stop!"

Marsh had grabbed Maggie's broken arm and was yanking on it as he tried to retrieve his shiv. The pain from the broken bones and the pins coming loose was sudden and excruciating. She screamed as he finally managed to pull the shiv out of the cast.

Marsh still had hold of Maggie's arm and was about to strike again when Crispin tackled him. Marsh tried to maintain his grip and Maggie was dragged halfway across the table before he lost his hold and hit the floor face first with Crispin on top of him. Marsh struggled but Crispin subdued him.

Thomas and Willis jostled to be first through the door. Dexter followed.

"Can I have a hand here?" Crispin snapped.

Willis put handcuffs on Marsh while a frantic Thomas asked Maggie, "Are you all right?"

Maggie was trying not to scream again from the pain. It felt warm and wet beneath the cast. She saw black spots in front of her eyes. Her legs buckled and she fainted.

She came to being wheeled on a hospital gurney. She heard someone yelling. It sounded like someone she knew. Maggie opened her eyes.

Giles Sumner was yelling at Thomas, who looked distraught. On her other side, Crispin was holding her good hand.

"Hang in there, Moppet. You did well, but now they've got to repair the damage Marsh caused. I warned you about the provinces."

Maggie gave a weak smile.

The gurney went through some swinging doors and her entourage was left on the other side. Except for someone who sounded familiar. He was saying, "Another nice mess you've gotten yourself into."

Maggie was about to correct the quote when an IV was put into her arm and a mask slipped over her face and she drifted off again.

Chapter 35

There were five men crammed into Maggie's hospital room. She supposed if she were a different sort of woman, she would enjoy the moment. As it was, she wished they would all just leave. All of them. Even her husband. She wasn't feeling well and all she wanted to do was sleep.

Unfortunately, sleep did not seem to be an option.

Not surprisingly, Tim was acting as spokesman.

"I watched the video. With sound. And it seems your earlier murders are solved. Correctly, this time. And I assume you now have enough information to identify the bodies you found without too many difficulties."

Dexter and Willis both nodded.

"And Marsh?"

"He finally asked for a solicitor. Who promptly requested a psychiatric evaluation."

"Yes. Well, prison or hospital for the criminally insane. As long as the man is locked up and can't do any more damage."

Maggie had to agree with that. And hoped Tim was finished.

He wasn't.

"And you," he turned to Maggie. "Why in heaven's name did you agree to be locked alone in a room with some lunatic?"

"And you," he pointed at Dexter and Willis. "How was it possible that this man had a shiv and no one noticed?"

Dexter and Willis studied their shoes.

"It's a good thing I sent Lennox along to observe," said Tim, a trifle smugly.

For a moment, Crispin seemed like he would also look smug, but quickly decided he would do better to study his shoes as well.

"And if you think that all's well that ends well, I suspect you should ask Lady Raynham about the well part of it."

Tim glared at the men who continued to look at their shoes.

"I have a few questions, but they needn't disturb our patient. Dexter, Willis, Lord Raynham, if you'd come with me for a few moments, please."

Maggie watched the men leave, and then realised Crispin hadn't been included.

He regarded her solemnly.

"That was bad, what Marsh did. He took a serious fracture and made it worse. Much worse. I thought your surgeon was going to have a fit.

"And I should have realised there was going to be a problem sooner. I'm sorry, Moppet.

"I'd been told Gloucester was a bit like the Wild West. By a former Lord Lieutenant. He claimed it was because it's so close to Wales."

Maggie smiled feebly.

"And how are you?" she asked.

Crispin shrugged.

"Were I still a departmental employee, I'd ask for two weeks in the Caribbean to recuperate. R&R. As it is…"

"Well, there's always Scarborough. The sea air is quite restorative. And it's off-season. I'm sure you could find someplace within your budget."

Crispin was taken aback, then laughed.

"You are a delight as always, my Moppet. However, you look like you should rest. And I'm not sure I want to be here when his lordship returns. So I will say not adieu, but au revoir. Tell Tim, should he inquire, that I'm waiting in the car."

He paused in the doorway. "And remember. Your Crispin is only as far away as *1."

He left.

Maggie was dozing when Thomas came in. He was alone. Even half awake, Maggie could tell he was not in a good mood.

Thomas couldn't help himself.

"Willis certainly seemed solicitous."

"Willis feels guilty."

"And Archibald-Atherton."

"I expect Lennox is equally solicitous with his mother. We must be around the same age."

That silenced Thomas. He knew whether he agreed or disagreed with Maggie about the age issue, he would end up in deep trouble.

"Well played, Maggie," she congratulated herself. And she was reasonably sure she was at least a decade younger than Crispin's mother. And, as an experienced tutor, she was also quite certain Crispin did not regard her at all maternally.

"But that's enough of that, Eliot," she told herself firmly.

Chapter 36

The following day, Thomas drove Maggie back to Beaumatin.

She stood in the great hall with its checkerboard marble floor and old oak panelling and ancestral portraits and looked around like she had never seen it before.

"Maggie?"

"Well, I've had it. People are going to have to take care of themselves from now on. And the snowdrops are on their own. And if anyone ever wants to arrest you again, William will have to deal with it. And if I'm bothered by a bad man, or by someone I even think is a bad man, I will simply shoot him. We can bury him in the garden. Or in one of the fields with the sheep. It worked for Marsh for a long time. And we're smarter than him."

"We?"

"I assume I would need some help. With burying a body. Unless we fed it to some pigs. I understand that's quite effective. Apparently they even eat the bones. Do you know anyone who keeps pigs?"

Thomas' mouth twitched. Then he looked at Maggie more closely.

"Maggie, are you all right?"

Maggie wanted to say she was very much not all right, but instead she said, "I'm fine. Just a bit tired. And my arm... hurts."

"Then go lie down. And I'll come up shortly with your medication."

Thomas found Maggie sitting on the edge of her bed in tears.

"I'm sorry. It must be an after-effect of the anaesthesia. I couldn't get my pants off. Or my top. I just hate being so helpless."

"You are one of the least helpless people I have ever known," said Thomas.

"So here. Let me help you. No. Wait. Take these first."

He handed her two pills.

"Two?"

"Maggie. Please. For once don't argue."

Maggie was about to argue that she didn't always argue but saw the look on Thomas' face and decided to keep quiet and take the pills.

"All right. Now stand up."

Maggie stood.

Thomas unzipped her jeans and slid them down. He became temporarily distracted by the chartreuse green thong she was wearing, and then decided he should focus on something else.

He slid her bulky sweater over her head and good arm, and then carefully pulled it over her cast. He paused.

"No bra?"

"It's hard with only one hand."

"You know I'm happy to assist. You have only to ask."

Maggie gave a tentative smile. "I know. Thank you."

The pain medication was starting to work.

With Thomas' help, Maggie crawled under the covers.

"Sleep, Papillon. I'll make sure you're up for dinner."

"If you have to wake me, could you please bring some coffee?"

"Of course."

Thomas kissed her, turned out the light and left.

Maggie slept.

Susan Alexander

Chapter 37

The next morning, from her study window, Maggie was surprised to see Thomas and Dexter drive off. Again.

"What now?" she wondered.

She went back to laboriously typing emails. Why was it so hard to type with one hand? Didn't Ravel even write a concerto for a pianist who had only one hand? His left hand? She would have to do a Google search to see if there were some technique she could use.

Thomas and Dexter returned just before lunch. Dexter drove off. Thomas came into Maggie's study and sat down on her sofa.

Thomas looked grim and Maggie felt a wave of anxiety rush into her stomach.

Thomas noticed. He got up.

"Come sit with me," he said.

Maggie felt even more anxious.

"It's all right, Maggie. Don't worry. It's just…"

She sat down. At the other end of the sofa.

"Dexter and I went to see Cedric and Beatrix. To tell them Charlotte's death wasn't a suicide. David and Chloe were there as well.

"Beatrix wept. I hadn't known… I didn't realise that Beatrix blamed herself for Charlotte's suicide. Or how badly Charlotte's death had affected Emily. How damaging it had been. They hope that knowing…

"Dexter told them he believed that at least the coroner's verdict could be changed from suicide. With Greenaway and Walker dead, and Marsh an accomplice at best, whether there will ever be justice in the legal sense... He couldn't make any promises.

"But Dexter said if it would help if he talked to Emily and explain, he would. He said he would even wear his uniform if it would make it seem more 'official.' I think that was his ultimate sacrifice," Thomas smiled and moved to sit beside her.

"Ah, Maggie. I know I called you a crackpot. And pig-headed. And forced you to use, er, subterfuge. But it's a good thing that you've done. Beatrix says you're a heroine. Again. And that she'll come see you later this afternoon, when she's had a chance to sort herself."

Maggie nodded. At the moment, she was just feeling empty. It did make her feel somewhat better that Thomas had his arms wrapped around her. And she could smell his citrusy spicy aftershave.

Unfortunately, he kissed her on the top of her head, stood and said, "I think Mrs Cook has lunch ready."

Maggie sighed. Lunch.

"She's fixed Welsh rarebit."

Well, that was all right. Maggie quite liked Welsh rarebit, a more complex, savoury version of cheese-on-toast.

After lunch, Thomas announced he was going out with Ned.

Maggie thought either Thomas' arm was healing very rapidly or he was taking stoicism to new heights. Or maybe it was even more irksome for him not to be able to do his Lord-of-the-Manor thing.

She wondered if she should do the Solicitous-Wife thing.

"How is your arm?"

Thomas shrugged.

"Really?"

"Better than yours."

All right. Well, she'd tried.

Maggie retired to her study. She opened her email programme and found seventeen new emails waiting. But her left hand was sore from overuse. The emails would just have to wait.

She retreated to the sofa with an academic journal, but it was hard to read holding it one-handed. She gave up. She knew she'd have the same problem with any recreational reading.

It was early afternoon. She was sure there was nothing on TV that she would want to watch and she had seen all their DVDs.

An audio book, then. But which? She certainly did not want to listen to a mystery featuring a murderous psychopath. Maybe...

Aha. Janet Evanovich. Stephanie Plum. Jersey girl. Another pig-headed crackpot. The stories made her laugh. Maggie vaguely recollected Ms Plum getting shot in a buttock in one book and reflected that there were worse things than a broken arm. At least she could sit and lie down without difficulty.

Maggie was dozing with the volume on low when Mrs Cook came in to announce Lady Ainswick.

Maggie struggled to her feet.

"Beatrix. I'm afraid I nodded off. Would you like some tea? Earl Grey? Let me wash while Mrs Cook brings some."

Maggie returned just as Mrs Cook came in with a tray of tea and coffee. Beatrix thanked her, looked at Maggie's cast and said she would serve.

Maggie thought Beatrix appeared to be less tired. Some of the lines on her face seemed less severe. She looked younger. Maggie decided that Emily wasn't the only one to have been devastated by Charlotte's death.

Beatrix began. "Thomas and that Scotland Yard detective. Dexter? They came by and told us this morning. That Charlotte hadn't killed herself. That it was Greenaway. And that Walker woman. With the help of Nat Marsh. That Greenaway had been stealing snowdrops and giving them to Marsh. And that Walker woman. And that Marsh had killed Walker, not Greenaway."

She shook her head.

"I can't believe I thought Charlotte would have done something like that. I blamed myself. Because of Edward. She had been such a sweet and happy child, until he…"

Edward was the Ainswicks' son. He had seduced Charlotte when she was sixteen and Emily was the result. And now both Edward and Charlotte were dead.

"And that Marsh. How could I have invited him to Rochford Manor? Such a terrible person."

"It was good that he spoke at your seminars. It gave us... "

Maggie quickly corrected herself. "Me a chance to find his secret garden. And confirm that he had the Beaumatin's Blondes and the Chloe Symeons and some of the other snowdrops that went missing from Rochford Manor."

"Yes. That Inspector Dexter says there's a good chance they will be returned."

"I think the police have finally begun to understand what these small white flowers are worth to their owners."

"But my dear. That dreadful man. What he did to Thomas. And to you. How are you?"

"I'm all right. It's bothersome to have the use of only one arm. And my left one at that. But I'll heal. And if what I did can help Emily..."

"Yes. You are a heroine. Again. As I told that husband of yours."

Maggie made a self-deprecating gesture and Beatrix looked at her closely.

They talked about the weather and the winter that did not seem to want to let go. And Chloe's pregnancy.

"She had a sonogram and they seem to think it's a boy. No more waiting and wondering, like Cedric and I had to do. If it is a boy, Simon Peevey will be undertaking the necessary legal steps so the child will be the next Viscount Ainswick."

Maggie knew that when Edward died, there had been no other males to inherit the title. However, the complexities of the process to have Chloe and David's child declared the heir were beyond her.

Beatrix looked closely at Maggie again.

"You look tired, my dear. I gather yours is not a simple fracture. And you've had to have two operations to mend it. Because of that dreadful man. So let me see if that husband of yours is around. I have some... horticultural issues to discuss with him. Did he tell you I think he should start selling some of the Beaumatin snowdrops? He doesn't have to open a shop. We can sell them along with our own. David thinks it's a splendid idea."

"I once told Thomas that after a garden tour he should offer refreshments and have tea cups for sale with pictures of all twenty-eight barons in presentation boxes. People could collect them."

Beatrix looked startled.

"I was joking, Beatrix."

"Oh. Yes. Of course you were."

She stood.

"Well, you rest. And let me see if Thomas has returned."

Beatrix found Thomas in the hall.

"Did you see Maggie?" he asked.

"Yes. And Thomas, if you have a moment, I'd like a word."

"Certainly. My study?"

They took seats in front of the fireplace beneath a painting by Dante Gabriel Rossetti of a woman with long, curly auburn hair. The woman in the picture bore a striking resemblance to Maggie.

Beatrix did not beat around the bush.

"Thomas, how do you think Maggie is doing?"

"Maggie? How is she doing? Why, all right, I suppose. Considering. It's what she says when I ask her. And I do ask her."

"Just what I thought."

"What do you mean?"

"Of course Maggie says she's all right. She always says she's all right. Even when she isn't. I would have thought you'd have realised that by now."

"But…"

"I think she's depressed. I didn't spend those last ten years with Charlotte not to recognise depression when I see it."

"Maggie? Depressed? But why?"

Beatrix regarded Thomas as though he were being very dim.

"You mean aside from being attacked by that terrible Marsh? Twice? And that she's doubtless in pain? And feeling helpless? At the same time she's missing a term at Oxford? Don't you think she's feeling a bit displaced? And useless?

And Raynham, don't think I don't strongly suspect you had something to do with the reduction in her schedule."

Thomas had to try hard not to squirm.

"So what should I do?"

"A normal man might take his wife on a Mediterranean cruise for a couple of weeks."

Thomas was taken aback.

"I'm not sure Maggie is the type who would enjoy a cruise. And I know I certainly wouldn't."

Beatrix glared at Thomas. He threw up his hands.

"All right. I'll think of… something. And thank you for calling this to my attention."

"Humpf."

Beatrix stood.

"I will go, as I am doubtless needed at home," she said.

Thomas saw Beatrix to her car, and then went back into the house. He paused outside of Maggie's study, then knocked and went in.

Maggie was sprawled on her sofa with an academic journal. She held it in her left hand and was using her cast to try to prop the pages open. Her eyes had shadows and there were lines around her mouth that had not been there a month ago.

Maggie saw Thomas and smiled. Thomas noticed it did not reach her eyes.

"Hi. Did Beatrix leave?"

"Yes. I just saw her off."

"She seems… better."

"Yes. And how are you?"

"Me? I'm fine. I'm all right."

Just what he expected she would say. What she always said.

"I'm trying to develop a technique to keep a journal open while I read. Once I've mastered that, I need to figure out how to make margin notations."

"I see."

"How are the sheep?"

"The sheep? They're, er, sheepish."

"To be expected, I suppose."

"They'd be happier if the weather were a bit warmer so there was fresh grass and not the same old and by now somewhat stale hay they've been eating all winter."

"Yes. I understand that's a problem for birds and bunnies as well as sheep."

Thomas nodded.

He leaned over, scooped up his wife, and sat back down with her in his lap. The journal slid to the floor.

"My dear, are you really all right? Beatrix seemed to think…"

"Yes?"

"Well, she thought you seemed... a bit... depressed."

Maggie sighed.

"Is she right? Are you depressed? It seems unlike you."

"Perhaps. A bit. Although it's equally possible it's the weather. Or too much anaesthesia. Or being so restricted."

"Is there anything I can do?"

Maggie snuggled closer to Thomas.

"Well, this is nice. But I realise it's not viable for the longer-term."

Thomas laughed. Tightened his hold.

"No. Regrettably, it's not."

"I expect I will just need to tough it out."

"Would you like me to take you on a cruise? Someplace warm and sunny?"

Maggie looked at Thomas in astonishment.

"No. Thank you. That's very kind. But no."

Thomas looked relieved.

"I didn't think so."

They sat quietly for a few minutes. Finally Thomas said, "Well, Papillon, I'm afraid I still need to wash and change before supper."

"Of course."

Maggie stood up.

Thomas kissed her on the top of her head and left.

Maggie decided she should at least check to see who had sent her emails. They were mostly work-related. One was from Malcolm who thanked her for her recent hospitality and wanted to know when he could expect her one-pager (or two) for her new book.

Maggie shook her head and replied, one handed, "Nice to see you as well. Door always open. Soon."

She checked some news sites and decided it was dinnertime and to see if Thomas had come down.

His study was empty but something on his desk caught her eye.

It was a photo in an elegant silver frame. It had been taken at the Snowdrop Ball. It was of her and Thomas.

The photographer had captured them returning from the dance floor to their table. She was in that dress. That extraordinary Ice Queen dress that fit her so perfectly and was so beautiful. But so cold.

Thomas was one step behind her. He looked magnificent in his white tie and tails. He was looking at her. His expression was tender. Proud. Loving. It was the way any woman who loved a man would want him to look at her.

Thomas found Maggie sitting with the picture in her lap and crying.

"Maggie. My dear. What's the matter?"

Maggie swiped at tears with the back of her hand.

"I'm sorry. I just... I just hope you're not disappointed. That I'm not the wife you wanted. Or expected."

"Maggie. I know we've had our differences... But of course you're the wife I wanted. I only hope I've met your expectations..."

Maggie shook her head. "No. I had none. Expectations. Well, having never been married... Just..."

Thomas took out his handkerchief and dried her tears with the white cotton square. He handed it to her so she could wipe her nose.

"Of course, at some point I might expect that you would occasionally have your own handkerchief."

"Sorry."

Thomas took the picture and put it back on his desk. Then he pulled her up.

"Come, my dear. Dinner is ready."

Thomas could tell from Maggie's expression what she was thinking.

"And no, it's not pie. I believe Mrs Cook has prepared salmon. And I have some of that nice Corbière that you like."

Maggie gave a final sniff and a tentative smile. That was all right, then.

Chapter 38

Maggie woke up in Thomas' bed and felt... better.

Maybe it was all the Omega 3's from the salmon.

Maybe it was because it looked like there might be some sun shining behind the still-drawn curtains.

Maybe it was Thomas. Could a husband be an anti-depressant?

Whatever it was, she did not feel like she had the previous day, when all she had wanted to do was crawl into a hole and pull the top in after her.

So. Time to rise and shine.

Then she grimaced.

She had forgotten about the ordeal of showering. Shampooing. Dressing. And the long, restricted day ahead where doing the simplest thing would be a challenge.

Well, so much for the brighter day.

Thomas came in with two mugs of coffee.

"Have some coffee. Then I'll help as needed. Even with shampooing, if you'd like."

Maggie considered his offer.

"Some help dressing would be appreciated."

If Thomas helped with her shampooing, she knew it would certainly not end there. And she needed to keep her cast dry.

"I'll give you five minutes. Then I'll come in," he said agreeably.

"All right."

When Maggie emerged from the shower, wrapped in a towel, she found Thomas had already made a wardrobe selection.

The pants and oversized top were unexceptional, but Maggie looked dubiously at the little bits of peach lace that were a bra and briefs.

"Well, they were in with your lingerie. I assume you bought them. With the intention of wearing them," explained a somewhat defensive Thomas.

"Gentleman's choice, then." Maggie smiled.

When she was dressed, Maggie went to get another mug of coffee from Mrs Cook, while Thomas retired to work on some accounting.

It was, in fact, a sunny day. Chilly, but the sun and blue sky were welcome.

Maggie decided she'd go walk around the gardens and grab some rays before she began to work on the proposal for Malcolm. Who knew how long the sun would be out?

The extended winter had had the effect of prolonging the snowdrop season. The late cultivars were still blooming and Maggie tried to see if she could guess which was which before referring to the label.

She was in the part of the garden where the snowdrops nestled among witch hazel—hamanelis—and birch trees. She was admiring the sherbet-coloured blossoms of Girard Orange when she saw it.

Maggie stopped. Stepped back and approached again. Could what she was seeing be a trick of the light?

She carefully circled the plant. Knelt down and with the utmost care lifted one of the small white flowers so she could better see its inner segments.

Oh dear. She had better tell Thomas immediately.

Thomas was at his desk and, from his expression, the accounting was not going smoothly.

"Thomas?"

"Moment."

He taped some keys and then hit return with some force.

"Thomas?"

"Yes?" Testy.

"Um, there's something in the garden. I think you should come and see."

"What?"

"It would be better if you saw for yourself."

"Has someone broken into the enclosed garden?"

"No."

"A fungus?"

"No. Or I don't think so. I'm not sure I'd...."

"And it can't wait?"

"No. And you know if it weren't important, I wouldn't have disturbed you."

Thomas sighed, saved his spreadsheet and stood.

"All right, Papillon. Let's go see this... whatever it is."

Maggie just hoped what she had seen was still there. And was what she thought it was. Thomas would be extremely cranky if this turned out to be a wild goose chase.

They had reached the area where Maggie had seen it. It was still there.

"Just look around. I want to see if you see it too,"

Thomas made an exasperated noise, then glanced this way and that.

"Really, Thomas. Look closely. Take your time."

He looked around more carefully. Became still. Approached.

"Is this what you mean?" he asked.

"Yes."

"Good God."

He knelt down and carefully turned one of the flowers up to examine its inner segments.

"Well, well."

He stood.

"My dear, it seems you have discovered a blue snowdrop."

"More like teal, I thought."

"Blue. Teal. It is certainly unique."

"Is it?"

"Absolutely."

"Worth being dragged away from your spreadsheet?"

"Yes."

"So what happens now?"

Thomas considered.

"My preference would be to leave it in place. Not disturb it until it's finished blooming. But given what you'd call the Zeitgeist…"

"It would be safer in the, er, secret garden?"

"Yes. But let me think about it a bit more. Before we do anything."

"All right."

They stood and looked at the plant. There were two flowers. The flowers had bright greenish-blue ovaries and the chevrons on their inner segments were the same colour, as were some fine lines at the tips of their plump outer segments.

"Will you tell Beatrix? And David?"

"Beatrix certainly. Although I doubt she'd have any better idea about whether it's safer to move it or leave it in place than I do."

"Oh."

"I have heard some people just remove the flowers. That would keep it safe."

"But I thought a plant needs its flowers. If you want plant, er, babies…"

Thomas shook his head.

"Well, remember I'm still learning," Maggie said in her own defence.

"Anyhow, let's go back. It should be all right for an hour or so. Loki and Freya can earn their dog food. And I'll warn everyone to make sure there's no one around who shouldn't be here."

Thomas put his arm around her.

"Lady Raynham, you have been here for only a single snowdrop season, and you have discovered not one, but two new snowdrops."

"Beginner's luck?"

Thomas looked sceptical.

"Perhaps it's because I don't take what I'm seeing for granted. Since I'm still trying to tell which is which. So I look extra carefully."

"That could be it."

"Although I'm sure you would have noticed both of the ones I found. If you hadn't been doing accounting."

Thomas grimaced at the mention of accounting.

Maggie was going to ask if he couldn't delegate some of the work he did, and then remembered that he hated having nothing to do as much as she did.

306

"So what are you going to name it?" Thomas asked.

"Name it?"

"Generally the person who finds a new snowdrop gets to name it."

"Oh."

Maggie thought. The colour reminded her somewhat of Thomas' eyes. Of course, Thomas' eyes were much more variable. And certainly affected her in ways the snowdrop did not. She wondered if that meant she was not really a true galanthophile.

She briefly considered Beaumatin's Thomas, but that seemed overly familiar. And she wasn't sure Thomas would care for it. Were there alternatives?

"Beaumatin's Baron," she said finally.

"Beaumatin's Baron?"

"Well, there are twenty-eight of you. And it's blue. Or blue-ish. And blue eyes seem to run in the baronage, if that's the right term. Not just you, but William and even young Harry. So…"

"Beaumatin's Baron."

"I thought you wouldn't care for Beaumatin's Thomas."

"You're right, Papillon. I wouldn't."

"So Beaumatin's Baron it is?"

"Beaumatin's Baron it is."

They began to walk back to the house. Thomas had his arm around Maggie's shoulders.

Suddenly Maggie stopped.

"Oh dear."

Thomas raised his eyebrows inquiringly.

"You remember when I came back from the hospital, I stated unequivocally that the snowdrops would have to look after themselves?"

Thomas thought. "I seem to recall that statement."

"Well, I hope that the Baron can take care of himself. Itself."

"I will put it in our 'secret garden' and install retinal scanners. And laser alarms. And motion detectors. And we already have Freya and Loki. And Ned and Jamie and Ian and Wesley. And I am sure even Mrs Cook would take up arms…."

To which Maggie replied, "Humpf."

GNAT

About the author

A native New Yorker, Susan Alexander lives in Luxembourg, where she writes and undertakes research on public policy and the social sciences.

She enjoys writing about women who have led complex and interesting lives, their relationships and the choices they have made. It frequently happens that there is some murder and mayhem involved as well.

Printed in Great Britain
by Amazon